# THE NEW AMERICANS

*A Cambodian refugee girl with her new doll in Oklahoma City*

# THE NEW AMERICANS;

*Changing Patterns in*
*U.S. Immigration.*

Brent Ashabranner

Photographs by
Paul Conklin

DODD, MEAD & COMPANY, C/983.
New York

1  2  3  4  5  6  7  8  9  10

Library of Congress Cataloging in Publication Data

Ashabranner, Brent K., date
The new Americans.

Includes index.
Summary: Discusses the immigration policies and
patterns of the United States, emphasizing case histories
of people from various countries and walks of life who
have come to this country seeking a better quality of life.
1. United States—Emigration and immigration—
Juvenile literature. [1. United States—Emigration and
immigration—History.  2. United States—Emigration and
immigration—Personal narratives]  I. Conklin, Paul, ill.
II. Title.
JV6455.A89  1983        325.73        82-45999
ISBN 0-396-08140-1

# CONTENTS

# Author's and Photographer's Note

We traveled more than ten thousand miles and saw a great deal of America in gathering the material for this book. The help we received from many people along the way was invaluable; the good will we encountered was heartwarming. At the risk of some unfortunate omission, we would like to express our appreciation to the following persons: Thao Bounlieng, Leon F. Bouvier, H. M. Calvert, Don Cassidy, Peter Chow, Mona Fikry, Mark Franken, Tesfa Ghebremarian, Alfred H. Giugni, David Glascoe, Ira Goetz, Donald Granados, Mark Handelman, Fr. Michael Hann, Christine McCollum, Mary Catherine Myers, Robert H. Neal, Jane O'Brien, Diane Schutee, Al Velarde, Rev. Thomas Wenski, Sister Anne Wisda.

In every city we visited we found a dynamic Catholic refugee resettlement program. These programs, run by the local dioceses under the general direction of the U.S. Catholic Conference, are rendering crucial help to the U.S. government in refugee resettlement. The remarkably dedicated staffs of these programs deserve a very special salute.

Our demographic research was greatly facilitated by numerous publications of the Population Reference Bureau in Washington, D.C. Particularly useful were their bulletins *International Migration: Yesterday, Today, and Tomorrow* and *U.S. Population: Where We Are; Where We're Going.*

*Brent Ashabranner*
*Paul Conklin*

# I

# A NATION
# OF IMMIGRANTS

*immigrant:* a person who comes to a country
to take up permanent residence

*Webster's New Intercollegiate Dictionary*

*Sue Lee today. She is assistant administrator in the Chinatown Manpower Training Project, a program which trains immigrants in New York City.*

T HE LITTLE Chinese girl sat quietly in a chair in the
Pan American Airlines office at Kennedy International
Airport in New York. A neatly lettered cardboard tag
pinned to her blouse read: "My name is Sue Lee. I am eight
years old. I do not speak English." The tag also gave the name
and telephone number of her father in New Jersey.

Sue Lee had flown from Hong Kong by herself. An air-
line stewardess who spoke Chinese had helped her through
immigration and customs. Her mother in Hong Kong had told
her that her father would meet her at the airport, but when
the stewardess led her out of the restricted area, no one was
waiting for her.

The stewardess took her to the Pan American office and
called the number on her tag. When she hung up, the stewardess smiled at Sue and said, "There was a mistake. Your
father thought you were coming tomorrow. He will be here
in an hour."

Sue sat in the chair and waited. She was not really afraid,

but she knew the funny feeling in her stomach would not go away until her father came for her. She had no memory of her father. Just after she was born, he had had a chance to go to America, and he had gone. That was eight years ago. Sue, her sister, and their mother stayed in Hong Kong, waiting for the chance to join him. Then Sue's chance had come, but she had to go alone. Her mother and sister would come later in the year. There was something about visas and passports that she did not understand.

The flight from Hong Kong had been long and tiring, and thinking about these things made Sue sleepy. Her eyes closed.

Sue awoke suddenly. She had not heard the office door open, but now a man was standing in front of her. Sue looked at him and thought she recognized him from pictures she had seen.

"Are you my father?" she asked.

The man smiled and bent down to pick her up. "I am your father," he said.

T H E   S U N was hot and almost directly overhead, but Mr. Wu did not mind. He sat in a back row of the chairs that had been arranged in the college quadrangle for commencement exercises. There were hundreds of people in front of him, but by sitting very straight and moving his head a bit to one side, he could just see the commencement stage.

He watched and applauded politely as the black-gowned young men and women marched across the stage to receive their diplomas, but it was easy to applaud and still let his mind wander back in time. It had been ten years ago that he and his wife and five children had come to America. His son James, who was graduating today, had been eleven years old then.

It had not been an easy decision to leave the Southeast Asian country of Malaysia, where their families had lived for generations. Millions of Chinese lived in Malaysia, but it was a Muslim country and prejudice against Chinese was sometimes strong. Both Mr. Wu and his wife were sure that their children would always be held back in Malaysia in some ways because they were Chinese.

Finally they decided to immigrate to the United States. They had been approved for immigrant visas after only a two-year wait because Mr. Wu was an experienced hospital technician in blood analysis. It had not been easy for Mr. and Mrs. Wu to start over in America at their age. But at least finding a good hospital job in New York had not been hard. Both Mr. Wu and his wife had become naturalized American citizens.

For the children it had been good. Their oldest son had graduated from the Massachusetts Institute of Technology and was now an architect in California. Their only daughter had taken a master's degree in public and private management at Yale and had just gone to work for a big insurance company. James had been accepted for medical school at Georgetown University in Washington, D.C. The twins would start to college in the fall.

"James Wu," the announcer called.

As his son crossed the stage and shook the dean's hand when he received his diploma, Mr. Wu smiled. And he clapped just a little louder, as he had seen the other Americans around him do when their sons and daughters crossed the stage.

THE BOAT seemed to fall sideways into a deep trough of waves. It shuddered when it fell and a wall of water rushed over the deck. People on deck, twice as many as the small fishing craft should have been carrying, screamed and prayed aloud.

Augustin shook the seawater out of his eyes and gripped the starboard rail more tightly. In the end, he knew, even a grip of iron would not help him. He had worked on boats and sailed on them for years, and he was sure this boat was in mortal trouble. He was glad there were no children in this boatload of refugees from Cuba.

The end came sooner than he had expected. Another angry wave hit the boat, and the ancient vessel seemed to crack in the middle. Augustin was flung overboard and into the cold sea. His only thought was to get away from the boat before it sank. He was a good swimmer, but now the sea simply swept him away. His only effort was to keep his head above water, to breathe. Once when he was pitched up by a wave, he thought he saw land in the distance, but he knew that it was probably just his mind creating fantasies.

Time passed and the sea did not take him under. It seemed to Augustin that he could swim now, and he did. But he did not know if he was swimming in the right direction or if it made any difference. He did not see anything again that looked like land. But he saw other things. He saw his mother. He saw his best friend and remembered saying to him just the week before, "I would rather be dead than live in Cuba under Castro any longer." It seemed now that he would get his wish.

He saw his cousin who had escaped to America years ago and who had tried to get Augustin to escape. It seemed to Augustin that his cousin was shouting to him to keep swimming, that he was almost there.

And then Augustin remembered nothing more and felt nothing more. The next thing he knew, his eyes were open and he was looking at a large pair of shoes. He was lying on cold, wet sand. His eyes traveled upward, and he saw a big American standing over him.

"Donde?" Augustin whispered, and then tried to remember his few words of English. "Where am I?"

The big American bent over and helped Augustin to his feet. "You're in Key West, Florida," the man said, "and you're mighty lucky to be alive, young fella."

THE CHINESE GIRL, the man from Malaysia, and the young Cuban are all very different, yet all have something in common. They have come to live in the United States, to make new lives for themselves in a new country. They are all immigrants, even Augustin, who will be given legal status to stay in the United States once the immigration court has decided that he is truly a political refugee.

Sue Lee, Mr. Wu, and Augustin represent the three major reasons under immigration law today why people from other countries are allowed to come to the United States to live: (1) to unite families, like Sue and her parents, (2) to bring in job skills that are needed in the United States, like Mr. Wu, (3) to escape political or religious persecution, like Augustin.

These three immigrant cases also illustrate a changing immigration pattern of recent years that is potentially of great importance to the United States. Far larger numbers of people from Asia and the Latin America-Caribbean area are coming to this country than have ever come before. They are coming as regular immigrants approved by our embassies overseas, as refugees fleeing from political turmoil or persecution, and as illegal aliens slipping into the United States because they cannot get permission to come.

In the pages ahead, we will look at the dramatic changes taking place in immigration and at what these changes may mean to our country. But to better understand what is happening today and what may happen in the future, we must begin with a look at immigration history.

# The Populating of America

THE UNITED STATES has been called a nation of immigrants and with good reason. Consider:

—The original thirteen colonies from which our modern nation began were settled by immigrants from England and a few other European countries. For almost one hundred years after nationhood immigration into the United States was completely unrestricted. Anyone who had the will and the means could come here to live.

—The black population of America is mainly the result of the forced immigration of the slave trade.

—Since it became a nation over 50 million people have immigrated to the United States.

—To this day about two-thirds of all legal immigrants worldwide come to the United States.

One of the most famous monuments in the world is the Statue of Liberty. The gigantic statue was given to the United States by France to symbolize America's historic welcome to

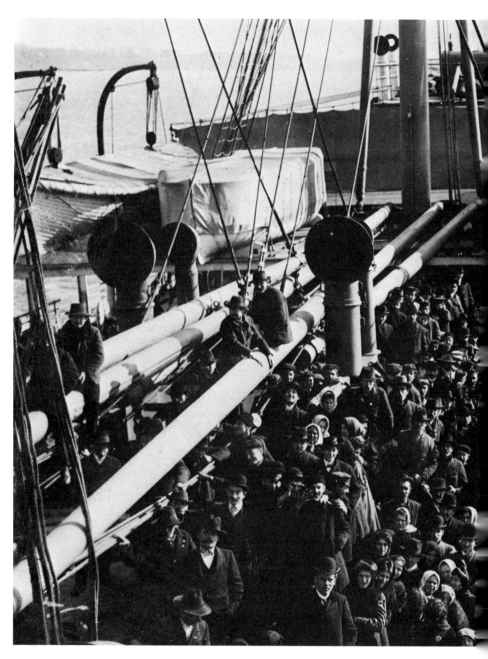

*Immigrants are crammed aboard this ship bringing them to the United States about the turn of this century.*

immigrants coming to the New World. The Statue of Liberty was erected on Bedloe's Island—now named Liberty Island—in New York Harbor and faces toward Europe. It was dedicated in 1886 by President Grover Cleveland.

Until recent years Europe was the primary source of immigrants to the United States. The fifty years from 1881 to 1930 saw the greatest flow of immigrants to this country, and the Statue of Liberty was the first sight that millions of Europeans had of what was to be their new homeland. Even if they could not read Emma Lazarus's poem cast in bronze on the Statue, they must have felt its meaning as they sailed close to the great lady holding her torch of liberty aloft. The poem concludes:

> Give me your tired, your poor,
> Your huddled masses yearning to breathe free,
> The wretched refuse of your teeming shore.
> Send these, the homeless, tempest-tossed to me.
> I lift my lamp beside the golden door.

While people in all periods have immigrated to America to escape political turmoil or persecution in their countries, a large majority, especially in the nineteenth and early twentieth centuries, came for economic reasons. They saw the United States as a new land of opportunity. They believed it could offer them jobs, land, homes, and education that the countries they left could not. The "golden door" they wanted to open was one that would lead to a better, more abundant life for them and their children.

According to U.S. Immigration and Naturalization Service figures, over 36 million Europeans immigrated to the United States between 1820 and 1976. Here is the breakdown of countries from which the largest number of European immigrants have come:

| | |
|---|---|
| Germany | 6,960,000 |
| Italy | 5,278,000 |
| Great Britain (England, Scotland, Wales) | 4,863,000 |
| Ireland | 4,722,000 |
| Austria and Hungary | 4,313,000 |
| Russia (U.S.S.R.) | 3,362,000 |
| Sweden | 1,270,000 |
| Norway | 856,000 |
| France | 744,000 |
| Greece | 638,000 |

Other European countries from which substantial numbers of persons have immigrated to America include Portugal, Denmark, Netherlands, Switzerland, Spain, Belgium, Romania, Czechoslovakia, Yugoslavia, Bulgaria, and Finland.

According to a Census Bureau survey, over 51 million Americans trace their ancestry to Germany. Those Americans of Irish ancestry form the next largest group, almost 44 million, followed by 40 million who claim English ancestors.

From the very beginning, of course, people have immigrated to the United States from other parts of the world besides Europe. In the mid-nineteenth century a small but significant number of Chinese and Japanese began to immigrate to America. They worked as laborers in the newly discovered gold fields of the West and on the transcontinental railroads then being built. They became migrant farm laborers and worked in laundries, restaurants, and other service establishments in cities.

Their numbers were never large compared to immigrants

*Reproduced from the Collections of the Library of Congress*
*Newly arrived immigrants at Ellis Island*

from Europe, but in 1882 the fear of a "yellow peril" of un-
controlled immigration from the Orient caused labor and other
groups to press Congress for action. The result was the
"Chinese Expulsion Act," the first piece of legislation restrict-
ing U.S. immigration because of race or country of origin.
This act did not call for the deportation of Chinese already in
the country, as the title suggests, but it did bring about a halt
to Chinese immigration into the country.

In 1917 Congress established an "Asiatic Barred Zone"
which prohibited immigration into the United States of any
person born in China, Japan, India, Burma, Siam (Thailand),
the Malay States, and the East Indies. The legislation even

barred natives of the Hawaiian Islands. In 1943, quotas were set up permitting very small numbers of Asians to apply for immigration to the United States. The figure for China was 105 persons per year!

During the first decade of the twentieth century, immigration from Italy, Russia, and other southern and eastern European countries was very heavy. If that pattern of immigration had continued, persons of southern and eastern European ancestry in the United States might eventually have outnumbered those of northern and western European ancestry.

The Congress of 1924 decided that should not happen. In the Immigration Act of 1924 Congress put a limit on immigration from European countries. The limit took the form of a quota system which made certain that many more immigrants could come from northern and western Europe—Great Britain, Ireland, Germany, Netherlands, Scandinavia—than from southern and eastern Europe—countries like Italy, Poland, Russia. About 84 percent of the quota went to northern and western European countries and about 14 percent to those of southern and eastern Europe.

The theory behind this highly discriminatory legislation seemed to be that the "ethnic balance" of the United States should be maintained as it was at that time. Most Americans in 1924, as today, could trace their ancestry to northern and western European countries, and the quota system that was developed insured that it would stay that way.

"All of our people all over the country," President Franklin D. Roosevelt once said, "except the pure-blooded Indians, are immigrants or descendants of immigrants, including even those who came over here on the *Mayflower*."

Of course what Mr. Roosevelt said is true. We are indeed

*Immigrants await entry into the United States at Ellis Island.*

a nation of immigrants. But it would be more accurate to say that we are a nation of immigrants mostly from Europe and most especially from northern and western Europe.

Immigration law changes, however, and world events cause different people to migrate. Major changes were on the horizon as the twentieth century progressed.

# The Golden Door Opens Wider

D URING the Great Depression of the 1930s immigration to the United States diminished to a trickle. America was no longer seen as the land of opportunity. Almost the whole world was in a depression. Many people who would have come to America despite the hard times were too poor to pay their passage. In the ten-year period between 1931 and 1940 only about half a million immigrants came to the United States, compared to an average of over 6 million in each of the three earlier decades of the century. After World War II, however, immigration to the United States began to increase again, slowly at first, then more rapidly in the 1950s.

World War II brought the United States into a closer relationship with the rest of the world, and it changed the way Americans looked at other countries and people. After the war many Americans began to question the racism and prejudice against certain nationalities that had become a part of U.S. immigration policy. President Eisenhower urged changes in immigration law to "get the bigotry out of it." President Kennedy said that quotas based on race and country of origin were "without basis in either logic or reason."

In 1965 a major new immigration law brought such racial and ethnic quotas to an end. The number of immigrants to the United States continued to be limited but in ways quite different from the past. Although there have been some changes in the landmark 1965 law, it is the basis for the present law. The main features of U.S. immigration law today are these:

—No person can be refused immigrant status to the United States because of race or nationality.

—The total number of immigrants worldwide is limited to 270,000 per year. Minor children and parents of legal immigrants already in the country do not count against this 270,000 limit.

—Refugees from political or religious persecution are limited to 50,000 per year, but this limit can be raised by the President. Refugees do not count against the 270,000 regular immigrant limit.

—Immigrants from any single country are limited to 20,000 per year. Refugees and minor children and parents joining legal immigrants already in the United States do not count against the 20,000 per country limit.

—Regular immigrants within the 270,000 limit are selected according to these criteria: (1) family unification—married children, brothers, sisters; (2) persons with special occupational and professional skills that will be useful in the United States.

Changes in the pattern of immigration to the United States have been dramatic since passage of the 1965 law. During the years 1900 to 1930, Europe was the source of 80 per-

*With the fall of South Vietnam, many Vietnamese refugees such as this man and his son came to the United States.*

*An immigrant from West Germany. Very few immigrants from Europe have come to the United States in the past decade.*

cent of all immigrants to the United States. Only 5 percent came from Latin America and not more than 3 percent came from Asia during that period. Today 80 percent of all U.S. immigrants come from Asia and Latin America, about 40 percent from each of those two widely separated parts of the world. The number coming from Europe has dropped to about 13 percent.

The countries of Latin America actually never had been under a U.S. immigration quota system until 1965, but immigration was light from the Hispanic countries until the mid-twentieth century. Then deteriorating economic conditions in some of the countries, political problems in others, plus increasingly easy international travel and communications brought about a rapid growth of Latin-American immigrants.

The poor and overpopulated countries of Asia had been waiting for almost a hundred years for the golden door to America to open for them. When it did open in 1965 they rushed in. With the fall of South Vietnam to the Communists in 1975, followed by fighting and chaos in Laos and Cambodia (Kampuchea), an outpouring of refugees greatly increased the number of Asians coming to the United States.

Since 1970 Mexico has been the leading country of origin of legal immigrants to the United States, followed by the Philippines, Korea, Cuba, India, and China. Not a single European country has been among the leaders for over a decade. Compare the above list with the leading countries in 1900—Austria-Hungary, Italy, Russia, Ireland, Sweden—and it is easy to see the great change that has taken place in U.S. immigration.

# The Importance of Immigration to the United States

THE IMPORTANCE of immigration to the United States is obvious when we look at it from the standpoint of history. The men and women who fought the American Revolutionary War were largely immigrants or the children of immigrants. The ideas of human rights, government, and justice on which our Constitution is based were brought from England by immigrants. These ideas were tested and added to in America but their origin was Europe.

Our religions were brought here by immigrants. Our traditions of religious freedom, tolerance, and separation of church and state were fostered by the Protestants and Catholics who had suffered religious persecution in Europe. We are an English-speaking nation, but our language has been enriched by thousands of words from the Spanish, German, Italian, and other languages which were the mother tongues of immigrants to America. Even today Spanish is the mother tongue of almost 8 million people living in this country. German is the first language of 5 million Americans, Italian of 4 million.

The forced immigration of hundreds of thousands of Africans to America in the eighteenth and nineteenth centuries profoundly affected our history. This immigration led to the nation's Civil War. It has also kept questions of human dignity and civil rights in the forefront of our national thinking and conscience as the large black minority has struggled to take its rightful place in America. The 26.5 million people in the United States who can trace their ancestral roots to Africa make this country one of the largest black nations in the world. Of forty-five black African nations, only Nigeria, Ethiopia, and Zaire have larger black populations than the United States.

Immigration has played a fundamental role in shaping the national character of the United States. We cannot today be accurately described as a WASP (White Anglo-Saxon Protestant) nation. Tens of millions of black Americans, Catholics and Jews from Europe, Asian immigrants, as well as our Latin-American heritage, have seen to that.

Neither is the United States a "melting pot" in which immigrants and their descendants have mixed together to produce Americans who all look alike, think alike, talk alike, eat alike. The melting pot concept is accurate, however, in the sense that over time the people who live permanently in the United States—those born here, naturalized citizens, legal and illegal aliens—are brought together in many ways. They are under the same government and subject to the same laws. They share ideas about freedom and responsibility. They work together. Their children go to the same schools. They watch the same television programs, read the same newspapers, enjoy the same sports, go to the same places of worship. Most speak English, though millions have learned it as a second language.

*This photograph, taken at a parade in Washington, D.C., shows how diverse America's people have become.*

But most ethnic groups in America—Italians, Poles, Irish, Chinese, Koreans, and many others—have at the same time retained some of the customs and traditions of their or their parents' or grandparents' ethnic group. They enjoy its festivals, dances, and foods. Many have relatives in their ancestral country, and they continue to care about what happens to that country. Many still speak the language of the country, and in some cases their children speak it. Most large American cities have sections where one national group or another tends to live close together—Italians, Poles, Germans, Palestinians, Cubans. Some Chinatowns, like those is San Francisco and New York, are famous. "Little Saigons" and "Little Havanas" are now a part of urban America.

Judge Cruz Reynoso, Associate Justice of the California Court of Appeals and a member of the recent Congressional Select Commission on Immigration and Refugee Policy, explains our national unity in this way: "Americans are not now, and never have been *one* people linguistically or ethnically. America is a political union—not a cultural, linguistic, religious, or racial union. It is acceptance of our Constitutional ideals of democracy, equality, and freedom which acts as a unifier for us as Americans."

It should be said that many people do not agree with Judge Reynoso in that they believe the English language and our Anglo heritage have been powerful unifiers of our country. But there is general agreement that immigration has resulted in a U.S. population of great variety and cultural richness which today we look upon as a source of our national strength.

Arthur Burns, U.S. Ambassador to Germany and former Chairman of the Board of Governors of the Federal Reserve System, was an immigrant from Austria. Speaking of immigrants, he has said, "They enrich our lives and they enrich our vision. . . . They create new opportunities for us as well as for themselves and make this country richer and stronger in the process."

Today immigration into the United States is again approaching the high level of the early part of this century. As we have seen, 80 percent of the immigrants are now coming from Asia and Latin America. How will these new arrivals benefit the United States? What kinds of problems will they create? Let us take a closer look at the persons who are now coming to this country to live and at how they may affect its national life.

# II

## NEW AMERICANS
## FROM ASIA

*Chinese immigrants learn use of office machines in a New York City CITA Program.*

I N A Baltimore hospital a slender, brown-skinned nurse smiles and jokes easily in English with the elderly patient as she gives him his evening medicine. She emigrated from the Philippines to the United States just a year ago, but she has quickly adjusted to life in her new country.

P R O M P T L Y at 7:00 A.M. in Seattle, A. J. Kim opens his service station. Five minutes later the first customer drives his car in—a Volvo. Mr. Kim specializes in repairing foreign cars and is proud of his reputation for good and prompt work. Mr. Kim, a Korean-American, came to Seattle fifteen years ago. He worked as a mechanic for ten years and then opened his own service station-garage. Mr. Kim is helped by his brother-in-law and cousin, who have only recently come from Korea to live in America. They do not speak much English yet, but they learned to be good mechanics working for the U.S. Army in Korea.

A T  T H R E E o'clock in the afternoon Phung Duoc Hung dries his hands, hangs up his dishwasher's apron, and leaves the Palm Court Restaurant in St. Louis. He walks to the bus stop and catches a bus to a different part of the city where he has another dishwashing job at the Moon Gate Restaurant. Hung, a refugee from Vietnam, started work at 8:00 in the morning and will not get back until midnight to the small apartment that he, his wife, and four children share with another Vietnamese family. He does not really mind dishwashing, but he would rather be a farmer like he was in Vietnam. Farming was harder work than washing dishes, but he had time to enjoy his children and talk with his wife. Hung was drafted as a soldier in the South Vietnamese Army. When the Communists from the north took over the country, he became a refugee to escape being put in a "reeducation camp."

A T  T H E Oak Ridge National Laboratory a young physicist studies reports on an experiment in applying solar energy to agricultural crop production. The name tag on his white laboratory coat says N. R. Cho. He is a Chinese-American who came to the United States with his parents when he was fifteen. Only recently he has finished his Ph.D. studies at Pennsylvania State University, and just a year ago he became a naturalized American citizen. Cho is one of more than twenty naturalized American citizens originally from China who are working as scientists at the famous Oak Ridge, Tennessee, energy research laboratory.

A L L  O V E R the United States today people who have come from Asia to live permanently in this country are participating in almost every phase of our national life. Between 1970 and 1980 the number of Asians in the United States grew at the rate of 125 percent, more than doubling to a total of about 3.5 million or approximately 1.6 percent of the nation's population.

There are over forty countries in Asia, but by far the largest number of regular immigrants to the United States come from just three of them: the Philippines, Korea, and China in that order. China includes both the mainland People's Republic of China and Taiwan. The number of immigrants from the Philippines in recent years is in the range of 35,000 annually, Korea 30,000, China 20,000. Large numbers of people from each of these countries qualify as immigrants under the family reunification provision of U.S. immigration law. Even so there are long waiting lists, as many as 80,000 in the case of China.

A U.S. immigration official said recently: "We have case after case of brothers who have not seen each other for thirty or forty years and who lost touch for much of that time due to the lack of relations between the United States and China. Family reunification is the most human part of normalizing relations between our two countries."

The most dramatic rush of Asians into the United States, however, has been the refugees from Southeast Asia: Vietnam, Laos, and Cambodia. From the fall of Saigon to the North Vietnamese Communists in May, 1975, to March, 1982, almost 600,000 refugees from those three countries have reached the United States.

The arrival of such a large number of refugees in a short space of time has created many special problems of settling in and adjusting. The problems are made worse because few refugees have relatives in the United States to help them as most regular immigrants do. Further, a great many of the refugees from Southeast Asia are uneducated people, illiterate even in their own languages, and with no job skills that are helpful to them in the United States. The federal and state governments, schools, churches, civic groups, and individual sponsors are working on these special refugee problems, and progress is being made.

A closer look at some of the refugees and regular immigrants from Asia will make clearer just who they are, what problems they bring with them, and how they are becoming Americans and making their own contributions to their new country.

# The Refugees

THE COLLAPSE of South Vietnam in 1975 led to Communist regimes not only in that country but also in Laos and Cambodia. People in those countries who had served in the armed forces, worked for the government, or who in any way had opposed the Communist forces, were marked for Communist retaliation. That might mean being put in a "reeducation center" at hard labor. It might mean death. Anyone who had worked for the American military or diplomatic organizations was in particular danger.

Fear of death, imprisonment, and life under communism caused a mass exodus from Southeast Asia. Vietnamese fled in boats, many of them completely unseaworthy. Their destinations were Thailand, Malaysia, Indonesia, and Hong Kong. Untold thousands of these "boat people" perished in their frightening journeys. Their boats sank in stormy seas. They died from lack of food and water. They were attacked by Thai and Malaysian pirates, robbed of what pitifully few possessions they had, and killed if they resisted. When they reached land they often had to wait for days before officials would let them come ashore. Sometimes they were towed back out to sea by a naval ship and told to go to some other country.

Laotian and Cambodian refugees traveled overland toward Thailand, walking at night to avoid Communist troops, finding almost no food in the famine-stricken countryside. As they neared the Thai border, there were more soldiers to avoid, and there was the added danger of being blown to pieces by land mines. Finally, for the Laotians, there was the wide Mekong River to somehow get across. These were the "land people."

Once the boat people and the land people reached Thailand, Malaysia, or Indonesia they were put into hastily organized refugee camps. These camps were overcrowded and without sanitary facilities. The refugees lived in makeshift tents or hovels made of mud, tree branches, packing cases, and anything else that could serve as a roof or a wall. There was never enough food, and clothing and medicine were almost completely lacking. Death and despair were a constant part of camp life.

When the international assistance agencies began to help, conditions improved. The Red Cross, the Catholic Relief Service, United Nations agencies, and the United States government working through these and other groups brought desperately needed supplies, shelter, and organization to the camps. But life for the refugees was still hard, and there was nothing to do all day but wait and wonder what was going to happen to them. Thailand, Malaysia, and Indonesia were countries of "first asylum," poor countries that could not accept the hundreds of thousands of refugees permanently. So there began the long process of finding countries that would take the refugees for resettlement. Australia, Canada, several

European countries, and a few in South America accepted refugees and are still taking some, but by far the largest number have gone to the United States.

The process of moving refugees from the countries of first asylum to countries of permanent resettlement takes time. Most refugees have to wait for several months and many wait years before being accepted by a country. There are still tens of thousands of refugees in camps waiting to be resettled.

REFUGEE BOATS coming into Indonesian waters were often guided by the great flares of waste gas being burnt off by American offshore oil well and drilling operations. The flame could be seen miles away, and boats would steer toward it. When boats came in sight, the rig radio operator would notify the Indonesian navy that more refugees had arrived.

A young Vietnamese man in an Indonesian refugee camp spoke of seeing the flame from his boat. "We had been three days without food, two days without water," he said. "My mind was not right. When I saw the flame in the sky at night, I thought it was the torch of the Statue of Liberty. I had seen a picture of the Statue of Liberty many times. I thought somehow we had come to the United States."

The young man looked around the squalid refugee camp, where he had now been for two years. "But I am still waiting to see the Statue of Liberty."

# Escape from Saigon

THE REFUGEE flood began not with the boat people or the land people but with a panic-stricken airlift from the South Vietnam capital of Saigon. The end came with stunning swiftness in May, 1975, bringing to a close twenty years of war between North and South Vietnam. With the American war machine dismantled and largely gone, the Communist Vietcong broke the cease-fire agreement and moved south. The South Vietnamese Army fell apart, and within days Communist troops were at the outskirts of Saigon.

Frank Brown was there that May. He heard the guns, and he knew it was almost over. He had served two tours in the U.S. Army in Vietnam before returning to Saigon in 1972 as a civilian worker, and he did not need the grave-voiced announcer on the military radio station to tell him that the city was in mortal peril.

Still, Frank listened carefully, for the radio was advising all American civilians in Saigon to go to the airport for immediate departure from the country. For Frank that was not so simple. When Frank returned to Saigon, he had married Thanh, a Vietnamese woman who worked for the U.S. Army as an accounting clerk. Now they had an eighteen-month-old daughter. Of course they would go with him, but it wasn't as simple as that, either.

Thanh's mother and father lived in Saigon, and her father was a noncommissioned officer of the South Vietnamese Army. He would be a certain target of the Vietcong. Thanh also had eight brothers and sisters. Except for a sister who was twenty-two, they were all of school age, ranging from six to sixteen. Without a father their chances of any kind of decent life under the Communist regime would be bleak.

Frank and Thanh talked over the terrible problem with Thanh's mother and father. Since Frank was an American, Thanh worked for the American army, and her father was a South Vietnamese soldier, it was possible that the U.S. military would evacuate the whole family. Thanh's father made the final decision.

"Everyone must go," he said, "but I will stay. I am a soldier and I will not be a deserter."

Frank and Thanh argued with him. They told him the situation was hopeless. They told him that hundreds of high-ranking South Vietnamese Army and Air Force officers had already been flown out of the country on U.S. planes.

"I know that," Thanh's father told them, "but others have stayed, and I will stay too."

Nothing more could be said. Frank told Thanh to get everyone ready, and that was easy to do. They could take nothing except what they could carry in a small bag or put in their pockets. Frank went to an army depot where he had friends and came away driving a small military bus.

Early the next morning Frank got everyone into the bus: Thanh, their daughter, Thanh's mother, and her eight brothers and sisters—twelve people in all, counting Frank himself at the wheel. Thanh's father was with his army unit and did not see them go. They left behind everything they owned: their houses, furniture, clothes, a car. Everything. There had been no time to sell anything and no one to buy if there had been time.

Panic was rising in the city. Many shops were closed, and the streets were jammed. Everyone was streaming toward the airport, on foot, in cars, on bicycles and motorbikes. Many people were loaded down with bags and suitcases that they would never be allowed to take on a plane, even if they got on one.

What was usually a half hour drive to the airport took three hours that morning. Frank guided the small bus carefully through the welter of people and vehicles, trying without success to find streets that might be less crowded. Everyone in the bus was quiet. Now there was nothing more to say, and a numbness of grief and uncertainty held all of them in its grip. Even Tammy, the eighteen month old, was silent.

Only Thanh's mother spoke once. "Perhaps your father will still come," she said to Thanh and her other children. But the tone of her voice told them that she did not think that would happen.

American military police were on duty at the airport, and the confusion was not as great as Frank thought it would be, even though there seemed to be thousands of people there, all pushing and trying to get through the barriers. Frank had no doubt that he and Thanh and their daughter and Thanh's mother would be cleared for space on a plane, but he was not sure about Thanh's eight brothers and sisters. When he showed his American passport, however, and Thanh's papers showing that she worked for the American army, their whole group was passed through to the waiting area.

They arrived at the airport at noon and waited hour after weary hour for their departure turn to come. It was hot in the building where they were put with hundreds of others awaiting departure. Some of the men were in uniforms of the South Vietnamese Army. Everyone had to stand or sit on the floor; Frank held Tammy most of the time. There was nothing to eat, and the water fountain was hard to reach through the crowd.

Night came and they were still waiting. Frank could hear planes taking off, and he wondered if there could possibly be one left for them. He also thought he could hear guns, but that, he guessed, was his anxious imagination. By midnight most of the children were asleep on the floor from sheer exhaustion.

At 2:00 A.M. their call came. They left the building, Frank still carrying Tammy, and walked across the dark tarmac to a waiting airplane. Frank saw that it was a C-130, and he wondered how all of the people streaming toward it could possibly get on. He moved his group a little faster.

They climbed the steps and pushed their way into the plane. There were no seats, but the first people inside sat on bench seats along the sides. Others sat on the floor and some stood, holding onto straps. By the time the twelve of them got on board, only a little space was left, but they crowded into it and sat on the floor. The plane was packed with people, every inch of space taken. Frank knew that the C-130 was a workhorse, capable of carrying heavy loads, but he wondered if this one could really get off the ground.

And then Frank saw something that made him forget

even the fear of taking off. He saw that there were no doors on the C-130. They had been removed, and in the open doorways commandos were strapped, holding high-intensity flare guns. Frank knew from his earlier army experiences why the commandos were there and why they were carrying flare guns. The Vietcong were firing heat-seeking missiles at the departing planes, and the commandos would fire the high-intensity flares to try to put the missiles off course.

Can we possibly get out of here? Frank asked himself.

Now the engines of the plane were screaming. Now the C-130 was lumbering down the runway, and there was no more time to think. But there was time to feel and hear. Every shake of the plane's body, every tremble as it finally lurched into the air, seemed to course through Frank. Every whine and roar of the engines as they strained and changed pitch pounded at his ears.

But the plane was climbing, climbing, and if the commandos had fired their flare guns, Frank did not know it. They would soon be over the sea, he knew, and with every second the chances of being blown to bits by a missile were becoming less.

Then the C-130 leveled out, and even with the doors off, the sounds of the engines now seemed smooth and comforting. Frank closed his eyes. His body was wet with sweat, but he felt strangely relaxed. He thought he might even sleep for a few minutes. They were over the South China Sea heading straight for Clark Field, the U.S. Air Force base in the Philippines. There was nothing more he could do until they touched down there four or five hours from now.

Today, seven years later, Frank, Thanh, and Tammy live in an attractive brick house in the pleasant town of Ocean Springs, Mississippi, near Biloxi. Next door, in a house that

*Frank Brown and his family in Ocean Springs, Mississippi*

is a twin of theirs, live Thanh's mother, father, and six of her brothers and sisters. Her oldest sister is married and living in New Orleans. Her brother who was sixteen when he left Vietnam is a junior in college studying engineering.

Frank works as an electronics specialist for a nearby shipyard. Thanh works for the Catholic Social and Community Services in Biloxi helping in the resettlement of Vietnamese refugees. Tammy and Thanh's six brothers and sisters have adjusted beautifully to their new life in America. They speak

English fluently, play neighborhood basketball and other sports, and are doing well in school. Two of them represent their Ocean Springs high school in interscholastic mathematics contests.

It is, Frank sometimes thinks, a miracle that everything turned out so well. But the biggest miracle, he has no doubt, is that Thanh's father Hai is now living in Ocean Springs with them.

Hai was arrested almost immediately after the Vietcong swept into Saigon. He was put into what the Communists call a reeducation camp but which in reality was a prison where he spent two years at hard labor. When he was released, he had but one thought: to try to join his family even if it cost him his life.

It almost did. He escaped by boat, which nearly capsized twice in heavy seas as they struggled toward Thailand. The refugees had hardly reached Thai coastal waters when their boat was attacked by pirates. The pirates swarmed onto the boat, armed with guns and knives. They took everything with any value at all. The dental work in Hai's mouth contained a small amount of gold. It was ripped out with a screwdriver.

Hai's shirt was sliced to ribbons by the pirates in the chance that something might be hidden there. Nothing was, but even in tatters, the shirt was of inestimable value to Hai. He had received one letter from his wife and daughter Thanh while in the Communist prison. He had carefully written their address inside his shirt collar, and it was his one hope of finding them. The pirates left the shirt hanging on him, and he has kept it to this day.

The desperate refugees made their way to shore and to a refugee camp. Once there, Hai told his story to the refugee resettlement officials and showed them the address of his daughter in the United States. Four months later Hai stepped off a plane in Biloxi. His wife, his children, his granddaughter, and his son-in-law Frank were all at the airport to greet him.

It was indeed a miracle.

# Royal Music in Nashville

I N ITS June 6, 1980, issue, *The Tennessean*, a Nashville newspaper, carried announcements of two musical events. One, entitled "Gobble It Up," began, "Country music goes wild with an all-star roster of musicmakers tomorrow and Sunday at the first Wild Turkey Jamboree of Country Music in Columbia. . . ." The other story carried the title "Far Eastern Delights" and the first paragraph read, "The Royal Laotian Classical Dance Troupe bring pageantry and 600 years of history to the stage in a benefit performance tomorrow night in Goodletsville . . ."

A visitor to Nashville, which bills itself as the Country Music Capital of the U.S.A., might understandably have been mystified at seeing those news items side by side. Laotian classical dancing in the home of the Grand Ole Opry? Classical Asian music in the territory of Johnny Cash, Eddie Arnold, and Loretta Lynn? To which many Nashville citizens might have responded, "And why not? Good music of every kind has a place here."

As if to make this point, the Royal Laotian Classical Dance Troupe was invited to perform at Nashville's Centennial Park as part of the city's Century III Celebration of the Arts.

Classical Laotian dances tell the story of the creation of the ancient Laotian kingdom, the "land of a million elephants." The dancers are dressed in elaborate costumes, headdresses, and masks and enact the stories through their complex movements and gestures. They dance to the music of traditional Laotian string and percussion instruments.

There are many forms of popular dance in Laos, but these classical dances, created over 600 years ago, have always been reserved for the royal Laotian court. They were to be seen only by the king and his guests. For centuries the royal dancers and their families lived in the king's palace as a part of his household. The dancer's art was passed down from generation to generation.

This tradition ended in 1975 when the Communists came to power in Laos, dethroned the king, and ordered all cultural activities such as classical dancing to cease. The story of how the Royal Laotian Classical Dance Troupe came to Nashville begins at that point.

The leader of the dance troupe in 1975 was a young man named Eckeo Kounlavong. Eckeo's father and grandfather had been leaders of the royal dancers. Eckeo received his formal dance training as a teenager and then became a part of the troupe. Dancing was his whole life, and when his father died, Eckeo took his place as leader of the royal dancers.

Then almost overnight his life fell apart. With the dethronement of the king, it became clear that all persons close to him were marked for arrest. Eckeo talked the danger over with his fellow dancers and then made his decision quickly

*Eckeo Kounlavong, leader of the Laotian Classical Dance Troupe, with one of his masks*

and quietly. One night he and his mother simply disappeared from the palace.

The royal capital of Luang Prabang is in a lush mountain province of Laos. The journey to the border was difficult, and Eckeo knew that at any moment he and his mother might be arrested and put in jail. He had some money, and he bribed government officials and soldiers with it. His mother had jewelry and that went for bribes also. Sometimes he managed to get them past a guard or patrol simply by lying.

At last they reached the great Mekong River that forms the border between Laos and Thailand. On a moonless night Eckeo slipped into the river. His mother, who could not swim, was tied by a rope to his side. Eckeo is not a big man but his body is lean and muscular, a professional dancer's body, and for what seemed like hours he swam, using the river's current to help them. At last they reached the far shore and were in Thailand.

The Nongkhai Refugee Camp in Thailand is not a pleasant place, but for the next three years Eckeo and his mother lived there. In the first months following their arrival, a few other dancers from the royal troupe escaped from Laos and made their way to the Nongkhai camp. Eckeo discovered that there were other Laotian dancers in the camp, though they were not classical dancers.

Slowly an idea formed in Eckeo's mind. Why not reassemble the Royal Laotian Classical Dance Troupe here in the refugee camp? If it wasn't done here while there were still some dancers together, a lovely part of Laotian culture would be lost forever. Besides, rebuilding the dance troupe would be a way to fight the numbing boredom of life in the refugee camp.

The other dancers liked the idea, and Eckeo and the former members of the king's troupe trained the other dancers in the classical forms. Slowly, using every scrap of material they could put their hands on, the dancers and their families made the musical instruments, costumes, and masks that the dances required. Performances by the Royal Laotian Classical Dance Troupe became one of the very few bright spots in Nongkhai camp life.

Then came disaster. Fire swept through the camp destroying everything—every tent, every building, every poor possession of the refugees. And every costume, musical instrument, and mask of the dance troupe. It was a blow that might have brought an end to the troupe except for an American worker at the camp. On his own, he raised money for new dance equipment to be made, under Eckeo's supervision, by Thai craftsmen and seamstresses.

Over time the members of the dance troupe decided that they wanted to go together to their country of resettlement, wherever that might be, whenever it might be. They discussed the possibility with refugee resettlement officials. It seemed out of the question, utterly hopeless. There were seventy dancers, forty-eight families, 260 people altogether. Still, they hoped for the impossible.

Rumors are a cruel fact of life in refugee camps. Every day brought new ones. They were going to be sent back to Laos. They were all going to Australia next week. They were never going to be released from the refugee camp. They were going to be split into small groups and sent to many different countries. Hopes rose and fell, fears flamed and died, on rumors that were never true.

Then came news that was too good to be true. Even the most hopeful were afraid to believe it. The whole dance troupe and their families were going to the United States. They were

*Laotian refugee works on a Nashville assembly line.*

going to live in a big city called Nashville. They could take all of their costumes, musical instruments, and masks with them. No, they said, it could not be true. But this time it was.

The dream of the Laotian refugee dancers came true because of an enormous amount of work on the part of many people. U.S. government refugee officials had to believe in the idea and take on the mountain of paperwork it involved. The Catholic Refugee Resettlement Program of the Nashville Diocese had to accept responsibility for the entire group. That meant finding sponsors, finding housing, finding jobs, arranging for English-language training, and much more.

*Korean musician*

Members of the Nashville Church of Latter Day Saints agreed to sponsor a number of the Laotians. A person who sponsors refugees agrees to help them get settled, answer their questions, help with their problems, and stay in touch with them during the long period of adjustment. This is entirely a volunteer service.

Today the Laotian dancers and their families are well settled in Nashville, and other Laotian refugees are arriving because of the successful group already in the city. Over eighty Laotians work in the telephone assembling plant of Northern Telecom, a large telecommunications organization. The Direc-

*A Korean folk dancer performs in Washington, D.C.*

tor of Personnel for the plant says that the Laotians are good workers. They concentrate on the job and have a physical coordination that, for some of them perhaps, can be traced to their dancing training.

It has not been easy to learn a new job, a new language, a new way to live in a strange city. Still, the dance troupe has stayed together. They practice on weekends, and they give special performances in Nashville and other cities in the area. They dance when the Laotians celebrate their new year and on religious occasions. They are preserving a rich part of Laotian culture and are sharing it with America.

Eckeo, a man whose only job once was to dance for a king, is now a machine operator in a textile factory. He has taken this change with dignity. In the living room of his small duplex in a Nashville working-class neighborhood, he has placed an altar containing an image of the Buddha. Dishes with neat arrangements of apples, oranges, and grapes stand before the altar. And Eckeo prays every day, giving thanks for the good things that have happened and asking for the continued well-being of his dancers.

While the Royal Laotian Classical Dance Troupe is probably the most dramatic example of how Asians today are making a musical contribution in America, it is by no means an isolated example. Korean-American musicians perform at the annual folk festival on the Mall in Washington, D.C. A Cambodian dance group in Silver Spring, Maryland, gives regular performances. At the famous Juilliard School of Music in New York, 15 percent of the enrollment is Asian.

In a recent *The New York Times Magazine* article about how new Asian immigrants are making their mark on America, Robert Lindsey wrote:

"From Sejii Ozawa, the conductor of the Boston Symphony Orchestra, who came from Japan, to Yo-Yo Ma, the awesome Chinese cellist, to Myung Whun Chung, who grew up in Korea, came to this country to study at Juilliard and went on to become one of this country's most exciting young conductors and pianists, Asians have already become a major component of the classical-music world in America."

# The Most Gentle People

O F ALL the tragedies of war in Southeast Asia, the calamities of the Cambodians are probably the most terrible. When the Communist faction, called Khmer Rouge, gained control of the country in 1975 they began a campaign of death and destruction against their own people that can only be called the work of madmen.

It is estimated that over half of the adult male population of Cambodia was killed by the Khmer Rouge. Total deaths by massacre, starvation, and forced labor may have exceeded 2 million. Whole towns were erased from the face of the earth. Children were taken from their parents and worked to death. In one village there is a mass grave of 2,000 children. Piles of skulls were to be seen throughout the country: 18,000 in one stack, 38,000 in another.

Religion was banned. All Buddhist monks who could be found were killed. Statues of the Buddha were smashed to bits. Pagodas were burned or torn down. Representatives of all foreign governments were expelled. All assistance agencies like the International Red Cross, UNICEF, and Care were thrown out of the country. Imports of medicine were stopped, as were all other kinds of imports such as machinery. Hundreds of thousands of people were driven from the cities to starve and die in the countryside. Behind these insane actions seemed to have been some idea of purifying Cambodia, of returning it to a simple agricultural way of life.

After the Khmer Rouge was defeated by invading Vietnamese armies in 1979, outsiders were again let into Cambodia and the world could see for itself what had happened. A report from the International Committee of the Red Cross stated that its first survey team was not ". . . prepared for the devastation and human suffering they would see during the next few days . . . The once bustling capital was deserted. In place of the million or so people who had populated Phnom Penh before 1975 were a few hundred, picking their way through the garbage, destroyed furniture, and overgrown vegetation which littered the streets. Hospitals and schools had been destroyed, libraries stripped, and on the city's outskirts lay amongst other things huge mounds of cars."

The report continued, "Malnutrition was severe, particularly among the children and elderly and acute food shortages were reported in many parts of the country . . . There was little useful transport, no public services, no trade, and government administration had been completely dismantled . . . it was estimated that out of 500 doctors, only fifty-six remained in the country."

To escape this horror, tens of thousands of Cambodians fled from their country between 1975 and 1979 to take refuge in Thailand. Since 1975 the United States has given asylum to several thousand of the Cambodians in Thai refugee camps,

*Sponsors meet a Cambodian refugee family as it arrives at Washington, D.C.'s National Airport.*

and late in 1981 a large group of 500 arrived in Oklahoma City. About 200 were settled in the smaller nearby city of Lawton, while the larger group of 300 stayed in Oklahoma City.

In general U.S. policy has been to spread refugees over the country in small numbers on the theory that they would absorb American culture faster than if they were with large numbers of their own people. A different policy was adopted for these Cambodians because most were uneducated rural people who knew little or nothing about life outside the vil-

*Cambodian father and child in Oklahoma City*

lages where they had previously lived. It was felt that they would need each other for support as they learned to live in America.

The Catholic Refugee Resettlement Program of the Diocese of Oklahoma City accepted the responsibility for resettling the Cambodians. Sister Anne Wisda is in charge of the program; she and her small staff have resettled over 5,000 refugees since 1975. They expected the resettlement of the Cambodians to be by far their hardest assignment.

"But it wasn't," says Sister Anne. "They are the most

gentle people I have ever known and some of the loveliest. We housed them in apartment clusters of a hundred or so. We had to teach them everything—about stoves, plumbing, refrigeration—everything. They appreciated everything. They tried hard to learn and do things right because they wanted to please us. They always smiled and tried again and again. Some were depressed when they thought about their homes in Cambodia, the way it had been before the Khmer Rouge, but they were never angry. Just gentle people.

"And hard working," Sister Anne adds. "Many of the Cambodians were in poor health when they arrived here. They had nearly starved in Cambodia, and they had to eat grass and roots and leaves at night as they escaped to Thailand. We got them well here with good food and medicine, and then they wanted to go to work. There isn't a family now that doesn't have one or more wage earners. Some have two jobs. They are working as dishwashers and helpers in restaurants. They are on cleaning staffs in office buildings and department stores. They work in laundries, in lumberyards and storage companies.

"At night and on weekends they study English. Learning English is hard for them, maybe the hardest thing of all. But most are trying their very best to learn."

Listening to Sister Anne, you cannot help thinking about the hundreds of thousands of Cambodians who were slaughtered by their Khmer Rouge masters. "Perhaps they are too gentle," you say.

Sister Anne shakes her head. "They are gentle, but they are tough, too," she says. "These people have looked death in the face many times. They know how to survive. They will make their way in America, and I think the country will be better because they are here."

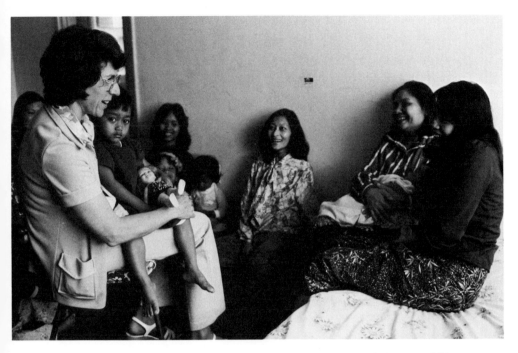

*Sister Anne Wisda talks with Cambodian refugees in their new Oklahoma City apartment.*

No one who knows Sister Anne would accuse her of being sentimental about refugees or unrealistic about the problems of their resettlement. In fact, she caused something of a national stir in 1982 with her comments to the press that a "welfare mentality" had developed among a majority of refugees who have arrived in the United States since 1978. They learn about the welfare program from refugees already resettled and from government workers, Sister Anne says, and many of them prefer to take advantage of welfare and put off taking jobs until their benefits run out.

Sister Anne's criticism is directed more at the system that encourages this welfare dependency than at the refugees who learn to use it. "We make cripples of good, strong people who should learn to work in this new environment, learn to be self-sufficient," she says, pointing out that the first Vietnamese refugees who came to the United States were very industrious and that most of them succeeded with little or no public assistance.

Sister Anne thinks that the government's recent decision to reduce welfare support from thirty-six months to eighteen was basically a good one, and she refers again to the Cambodians as examples of refugees making their place in the country through hard work.

# Homesickness

Y A T H O N G is a small man who, even when sitting in a chair, seems to be bursting with energy. His words come at you with machine gun rapidity, the English heavily accented but easy to understand. Ya Thong had medical training in his native Laos and served in the Laos Army Medical Corps. As a member of the military, Ya Thong was a marked man when the Royal Lao government collapsed in 1976 and the Communist Pathet Lao took over. Like tens of thousands of other Laotians, Ya Thong and his family of seven escaped into Thailand and became refugees.

Today, Ya Thong and his family are settled in a southwestern U.S. city and doing well. He is on the staff of the Vietnamese-American Association and works on the mental health and adjustment problems of resettled Indochinese refugees in the area. Through his medical training in Laos and his personal experiences in adjusting to America, Ya Thong is well qualified for his work. He remembers vividly and can talk eloquently about the terrible sense of helplessness he had upon arrival in what was to be his and his family's new home.

*Ya Thong, refugee from Laos*

"Not one word of English we speak then," Ya Thong will tell you. "I speak Lao and French but what good here? We were the first Laotians in this place. No one to talk to. Our sponsors are fine people and meet us at airport. We look and smile at each other but cannot talk. Person from Catholic Refugee Resettlement Program interpret, but he cannot stay always with us.

"We go first to sponsor's home. Big house, nice, many rooms but strange to us. They turn on television for children but cartoons frighten them. It is cold time of year, November, and sponsors have new warm clothes for children. But they have never worn clothes like these and are frightened.

"Then we go to house that has been rented for us. It is nice house and food has been put there by sponsor, but it is strange food and my family will not eat it. When we want tea, we cannot remember how the stove works. When the hot water tank went on, it made loud noise that frightened us and we think it will blow up. The phone rang and I pick it up and say 'Allo,' like I would in Laos, but voice at other end talks English and I do not understand.

"At night wind blows hard against the house. Children are scared and do not sleep. Everybody scared. In daytime we are scared to go outside because we cannot speak English and we may get lost. We stay in house and stare at each other. We are like in prison. My children cry and ask me to take them back to refugee camp in Thailand.

"I am husband and I am father, but I am like a baby, newborn. I can do nothing to help my family or myself. Sometimes at night I would think it is best just to die. All the time I thought about Laos and the home we had there and the friends we had there. When my children were not looking and my wife and her mother could not see me, I cried to be in my country again."

But, like so many thousands of other refugees, Ya Thong has a tough spirit inside his small body. Slowly he forced himself out of the house to shop at the supermarket and to go to other places his sponsor offered to take him. He studied English by watching television, listening to the radio, and using a French-English dictionary. A neighbor offered him some work as a carpenter's helper, and Ya Thong took it gratefully.

Then, with his sponsor's help, he got a job in a hospital, working on the wards. He forced himself to speak English at every opportunity, with anyone who would talk or listen, and his use of the language improved speedily. From the hospital job, Ya Thong went to work in an automobile factory and then to his present position with the Vietnamese-American Association.

For Ya Thong's children the terrors of strangeness began to lessen when they were enrolled in school and began to learn English, in which they had special tutoring help. "First day very scared," Ya Thong remembers. "Think they never come home again. But every day after that easier."

For Ya Thong's wife and mother-in-law the loneliness and isolation continued. They did not learn English. They seldom left the house. In Laos they had been dealers in the market and were used to busy lives. Finally, Ya Thong persuaded his wife to take a job in housekeeping at a Holiday Inn. Very little English was needed and she could learn from example. She learned quickly and learned English on the job at the same time. There was another position open at the Holiday Inn, and her mother decided to apply. She got the job and found that she could do the work, just as her daughter had. It was the beginning of a better life for them in America.

"But still I always think of home, of Laos," says Ya Thong, recalling those early years in America. "The second year we make a small garden in our backyard. Grow peas, peppers, cucumbers, lettuce, things like that. Sometimes in evening, after work, I see my mother-in-law standing in garden, just looking. Sometimes she touch a plant and I see tears on her face. I know she is thinking about her garden in Laos, just remembering.

"Homesickness is a terrible thing," Ya Thong continues.

"It is a physical thing. It hurts here." He puts his hand on his chest, near his heart. "You know, there are not many refugees in America today who would not go back to their countries if safe for them to go.

"Please do not misunderstand me. They are grateful for everything that has been done for them. They know how hard many people have worked to get them to America and help them live here. They know how sponsors and volunteers do this work for nothing. But the Afghan remembers his beautiful mountains, and the Lao remembers his green rice fields and at night they dream of them, and they hear the shepherd's flute and the boatman's song and they see their kinfolk and their friends that they left behind.

"With the children, of course, it is different," Ya Thong adds. "They will become Americans very quickly. Once they start to school, you can almost see it happening before your eyes."

A strange medical phenomenon may support what Ya Thong says about the power of homesickness. In the past few years a number of apparently healthy young Laotian men—as many as fifty by some reports—have died in their sleep at night. This mysterious occurrence has been called "nightmare death" and "sudden death syndrome." Medical science at present has no explanation for these deaths, but many Laotians believe that they know the answer.

"These young men cannot speak English, cannot get jobs," Ya Thong says. "Sometimes they have been resettled in cold states like Minnesota and Wisconsin. They have never seen snow before. They dream of home, of how they worked and were respected there. They dream of how it was warm and green all year long. Sometimes they feel they are not wanted in America, that they will never learn to live here.

They know they cannot go back to Laos, but they would rather be dead than not go back. So while asleep at night they die and their spirit goes back to live in their homeland."

Ya Thong spreads his hands. "Of course, I do not know if that is true, but that is what many of my people think. I do know, as I have told you, how terrible homesickness can be."

Thao Bounlieng is a Laotian who knows how very deeply feeling for the homeland can run. Thao worked for the American government in Vientiane, the capital city of Laos, so when the Royal Lao government fell to the Pathet Lao in 1976, Thao's life was in great danger, as were the lives of his wife and three children. One night, after careful arrangements for three small boats, Thao and his family, together with his mother and father, escaped across the Mekong River to Thailand. In time they were settled as refugees in Nashville, Tennessee.

With a good education and a good command of English, Thao was able to make a faster adjustment than most refugees to life in the United States and to help his family make a faster adjustment. Today both Thao and his wife have good jobs and the children are doing well in school.

Still, Thao thinks about returning to Laos. He says quite frankly that he would try to return if the political situation changed there, if his and his family's lives were not in danger. "But the longer I live here and as my children grow, there is less and less chance that I will ever return to Laos to live," Thao says. "I know that."

Thao talks to his children about Laos. "I tell them to be proud of who they are and where they came from. I do not think that will cause them to be less good Americans."

Thao has never met Ya Thong, but he agrees with him that most refugees would return to their countries if circumstances were such that they could. "They left their countries because they had to, not because they wanted to," Thao says. "That does not mean that they cannot live in the United States and become good citizens. I am sure most of them will. But they will never forget the land of their birth. I think any American can understand that."

# Shrimp Boats in Biloxi

T HE GULF COAST of Texas, Louisiana, Mississippi, and Florida offers some special attractions to Vietnamese refugees. It is warm much of the year like their native land, and there are jobs in seafood processing plants. More important for hundreds of refugees who were fishermen in Vietnam, a thrifty family can save its money, buy a boat, and become commercial shrimpers.

In the past few years many Vietnamese who were originally placed in other parts of the country have moved to the Gulf Coast to join friends and family members already there. In fact, only 5 percent of the Vietnamese refugees along the Texas Gulf Coast were originally placed there by resettlement agencies. All the rest have come from other parts of the United States.

There is no regulation against such "secondary migration." Once a refugee has been accepted into the United States he can live anywhere he wishes if he has the means to make the move himself. But sometimes a heavy concentration of

*A Vietnamese fisherman mends his nets in Biloxi, Mississippi.*

immigrants in an area causes problems, both real and imagined, and is objected to by people who have lived there a long time. That has been the case in several Gulf Coast locations.

As the number of Vietnamese fishermen increased in Gulf Coast communities, some native-born fishing boat owners complained that the newcomers were cutting down on the size of everyone's shrimp and crab catches. They were angered, too, by the fact that many Vietnamese fishermen did not understand local fishing customs. In Vietnam, for example, trawling is done from north to south, while in the Gulf the direction is east to west. This caused confusion and the fouling of lines until the Vietnamese learned "the rules of the road." They also had to learn about light signals, and they sometimes bumped other boats until they learned Gulf docking procedures.

More serious, however, was a feeling on the part of some that the Vietnamese presented a kind of unfair competition. They fished the way they always had in Asia. They would go out in bad weather if necessary. They fished long hours, into the night. They slept on their boats in order to get an early start. They used longer nets than was the custom in the Gulf.

One Gulf fishing boat owner charged unfair competition. "They've got husbands and wives, brothers, uncles, kids all working together," he said. "We don't do things that way. How can we compete with that? The answer is we can't."

These hard feelings led to trouble in some places. Vietnamese fishermen were threatened, in at least one case by the Ku Klux Klan. Seafood buyers refused to buy the shrimp and crab catches of Vietnamese fishermen. Docking privileges were cut back for Vietnamese in some cases. Sometimes this harassment caused the Vietnamese to move on to other places, but others refused to go. Trouble was nothing new to them.

Fortunately, the trouble has occurred only in a few spots and has tended to drop off in years when the shrimp harvest was abundant. Happily, too, some Gulf Coast communities have accepted relatively large numbers of Vietnamese and discovered that there was no problem that could not be solved. The small city of Biloxi, Mississippi, was one such community.

About 1,500 Vietnamese live in Biloxi today. Only about one-third of that number have been resettled in the city by the Catholic Refugee Resettlement Center, the principal refugee agency in the area. The other 1,000 Vietnamese have come

*Vietnamese refugee in Biloxi*

from elsewhere in the United States, most of them to join relatives already there.

"We like to have big family together," explains one Vietnamese man. "Brothers, sisters, cousins, uncles, aunts, children, everyone in one place. That is Vietnamese way. The American government did not understand that when they put us all over the country, just a few in many places. Now the families are coming together."

Shrimping and employment in seafood processing plants are the core work activities for the Vietnamese in Biloxi and the neighboring towns of Pass Christian and Ocean Springs. The plant owners appreciate the Vietnamese capacity for hard work and faithful job attendance.

"It is really hard to get anyone to shuck oysters anymore," one plant owner explains. "You try shucking them eight hours a day and you'll know why. But these people do it. They work hard and fast and they come every day. They are tops in this work. We have never had better people than they are."

The owner of a shrimp unloading dock calls the Vietnamese good, hardworking fishermen and absolutely honest. He says he does not think they make much difference in the income of the native-born fishermen because they are willing to stay out longer and work the poorer beds.

This willingness to understand and appreciate the good qualities of the Vietnamese doubtless stems in part from a deep-rooted American appreciation of hard work and sympathy for disadvantaged people striving for a better life. But the atmosphere of acceptance and understanding has been determinedly worked for by the Catholic Social and Community Services of the Biloxi diocese.

A booklet prepared and widely distributed by the Cath-

*A Vietnamese nun who works with refugee children in Biloxi*

olic organization explains to Biloxi citizens Vietnamese history and culture, as well as their recent tragedies. A line from the New Testament, Matthew 2:14, on the pamphlet's cover reminds the reader that as an infant Jesus, Joseph, and Mary were refugees fleeing into Egypt to escape Herod's persecution.

The Catholic organization, through its Refugee Resettlement Program, set up English-language classes for the Vietnamese, knowing that the ability to communicate was the surest road to harmony. Town meetings were held so that problems could be discussed and all points of view heard. Interpreters were made available when there was a special need. Materials on the rules-of-the-road in Mississippi shrimping waters were prepared in Vietnamese by the Catholic Social and Community Services and the Sea Grant Advisory Service.

The Biloxi diocese brought in two Sisters of the Most Holy Rosary from Philadelphia, one a Vietnamese who had become an American citizen, to assist the Vietnamese community and to do special work with the children.

"Who can resist these beautiful children?" asks Jane O'Brien, who is in charge of the Refugee Resettlement Program. "Sometimes when we take a group of them to a circus or some other entertainment, people think they are orphans. They come around and ask if it is possible to adopt them."

During the Vietnamese New Year holiday celebrations come special events like Tet Trung Thu or Children's Day. The children dance traditional dances, and in one of them invite the maid in the moon and the man in the moon to come down and give them candy. Television and other media coverage of such events has helped to make all Vietnamese

*Mr. Tran's boat being built in Biloxi, Mississippi*

more understandable and to be seen more sympathetically by native-born Americans.

But more than anything else, it is the Vietnamese capacity for hard work that has helped them win a place in this part of Mississippi. Mr. Tran is building a boat, the frame made of finest cypress. Mr. Tran and his family fled from Vietnam six years ago with no money or possessions, and they have worked very hard to save enough money for this boat. Mr. Tran has never built a boat before, and his son studying computer science at the University of Southern Mississippi has come to help him with the plans.

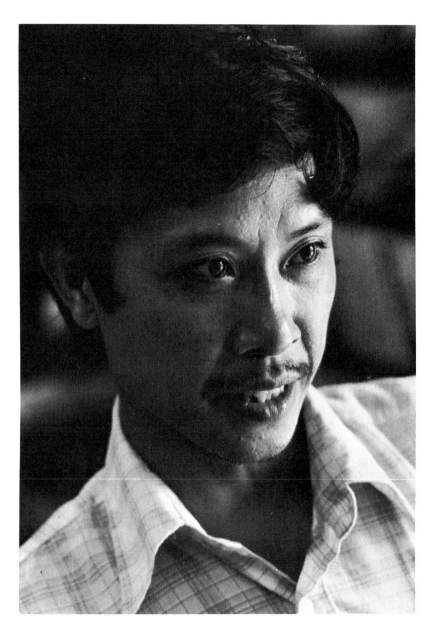

*Thua, a Vietnamese store owner in Biloxi*

Mr. Tran and his wife have eight sons and daughters. Besides the son studying computer science, they have two other sons and one daughter in college. They are particularly proud that a son in high school recently won a prize for his knowledge of Mississippi history.

By no means do all Vietnamese in Biloxi or anyplace else on the Gulf Coast work in the fishing industry. A survey has shown that perhaps no more than 15 to 20 percent earn their living from fishing or processing seafood. Many work in restaurants, others in motels.

"They work, save, invest in solid things," says Ms. O'Brien. "I know a tailor who now owns an apartment building and a gardener who has just bought a nice little house."

Some Vietnamese in Biloxi, like Thua, have gone into business. When Thua and his family first arrived in the United States, they were placed in Minnesota. Thua had a good job there as a machine operator, but his father was very unhappy in the cold climate. Thua moved to Biloxi for his father's sake; he found a job there, though not as good a one as he had had in Minnesota.

But Thua saw an opportunity in Biloxi. With the concentration of Vietnamese in the area, he felt there was a need for a store that could supply the kinds of things they used in everyday life as well as on special occasions. He got in touch with fifteen different members of his extended family around the country and asked them to put up what money they could to help him get such a store started. The family responded.

Today Thua has a very nice grocery and all-purpose store in a housing area where there are a number of Vietnamese families, although many people who are not Vietnamese shop there too. Thua calls his store an oriental grocery, and he stocks many products from Taiwan, Hong Kong, and else-

*Vietnamese refugee children at play in Biloxi, Mississippi*

where, such things as sweetened red bean paste, preserved Szechwan mustard, quail eggs, straw mushrooms, black bean paste, and a bewildering variety of noodles.

In addition Thua sells tapes with Vietnamese music, novels and other books printed in the Vietnamese language. He stocks bolts of cloth, tea sets, gold jewelry, costume jewelry, and of course such universally used items as milk, eggs, ice cream, and soft drinks.

Thua is doing well, and his success is a good example of

how the extended Vietnamese family helps its members. Of course he is expected to repay what he borrowed, and he knows that when other members of the family need help, they will call on him.

In April in Biloxi Vietnamese children pick blackberries from bushes hanging over fences and growing along the roadsides. In November and December they pick up pecans from yards and vacant lots. They are fond of berries and nuts and enjoy the free delicacies. In the spring their parents make gardens behind their houses, even in the tiniest space. They grow Chinese parsley, onions, garlic, lettuce, tomatoes, mint, and cucumbers.

The Vietnamese have found a place in this old Southern city of magnificant oak trees, lovely magnolias, and splendid houses along the beach road. The history of this city is not their history, but they will have a chapter in the next volume.

*Hyo Cha Yi and her daughter, Myong, in Alexandria, Virginia*

# "Education Is Everything"

EVERY WEEKDAY morning at 4:30 Hyo Cha Yi gets out of bed, quietly makes herself a cup of tea, and leaves her expandable trailer home, where her husband and three children are still sleeping soundly. Mrs. Yi slips behind the wheel of her 1973 model Chevrolet and drives the ten miles to Fort Belvoir, a military base near Washington, D.C. Even though it is dark, Mrs. Yi likes driving at this hour because the roads are almost deserted. When she learned to drive and got her license, she was terrified for months driving on the busy highways and freeways around Washington. She still does not enjoy driving but she is no longer frightened.

At 6:00 A.M. Mrs. Yi begins her job at Fort Belvoir. She is on the cleaning staff and works until one o'clock in the afternoon sweeping, dusting, and mopping in the base offices and other buildings. As soon as she has finished at Fort Belvoir, Mrs. Yi drives back to her trailer home, has a light lunch, and drives to her second job, which is at Bucknell Elementary School and fortunately not far away. Mrs. Yi is on the janitorial staff at the school; from three o'clock until eleven at night she helps clean the halls, offices, and classrooms.

Ki Chong Yi, Mrs. Yi's husband, also works as a janitor at a nearby school and he has other jobs. He is a part-time car mechanic and he works at Fort Belvoir when extra help is needed. Mr. Yi was a heavy equipment operator in Korea, but he has not been able to work at that occupation in the United States because he does not speak or understand English well enough and because of labor union regulations.

The Yi family immigrated to the United States from Korea in 1977. Mr. Yi had two sisters already living in the United States, so he and his family had a sponsor and could qualify under the family reunification provisions of U.S. immigration law. Even so, they had to wait for three years before their turn came under the quota system.

"My husband and I did not come to the United States for a better life for ourselves," Mrs. Yi says. She smiles and looks at the heavy push broom she is holding. "We had a good life in Korea, in Inchon, where we lived. We came to this country so that our children can get a good education. The very best education they can get. Maybe they will be doctors or engineers. Maybe they will go to West Point or the Air Force Academy."

Mrs. Yi speaks and understands some English, but when she is working at Bucknell school, the principal sometimes sends for Mrs. Yi's daughter Myong to translate or make clear more complicated cleaning instructions. Myong is eleven years old and in the fifth grade. She spoke no English when she arrived in the United States at the age of five but now handles the language like a native speaker. Myong has been placed in the gifted children's section at school and excels in both mathematics and art. She is a member of the school's safety

*Myong, a Korean, at school surrounded by her classmates*

patrol and was recently chosen "Outstanding Patrol of the Year."

Myong's older brother, who is fifteen, is also doing very well in school and like Myong is an excellent mathematics student. Myong's younger brother, however, is not living up to family expectations in school, and that is a source of concern for everyone. Myong thinks he is not trying hard enough.

"He flunked first grade!" she says indignantly. "How can anyone flunk first grade?"

The youngster, in fact, did not "flunk" first grade, but he is having some learning problems that are now being worked out. When these problems, not uncommon to foreign-born children, are taken care of, his teachers think that he will do very well. But in the meantime, the family worries.

"Education," Mrs. Yi says. "It is so important."

IN ITS ATTITUDE toward education, the Yi family is typical of most of the approximately 500,000 other Koreans living in the United States today and of most other Asian nationalities. Educational opportunity for children is one of the reasons most frequently given by Asian immigrants for their coming to the United States.

U.S. Census figures show that Koreans are one of the most highly educated ethnic groups in the country. According to one study of all U.S. residents who had completed at least four years of college, Koreans are at the head of the list. Here are the figures in percentages: Korean, 36.3; Chinese 25.6; Filipinos, 22.5; Japanese, 16.9; Whites, 11.6; Blacks, 4.5. The heads of households in one out of ten Korean families held either a master's or a Ph.D. degree. Of course, many Koreans and other Asian immigrants received their educations before coming to the United States, but the value they set on education is still clear.

Mrs. Freda Skirvin, a school administrator in a Northern Virginia suburb of Washington, D.C., with a high Asian population, has said, "Most Asian students I have seen bring an unusual degree of hard work, concentration, and interest to their studies. I don't know whether it is self-discipline, ambition, family expectations or all those things, but the result is academic accomplishment well above the average."

A young Vietnamese woman who came to the United States as a refugee at age fourteen graduated from the U.S. Naval Academy in the Class of 1982. Commenting on this, an Asian university professor said, "Except for freedom, educa-

*There are so many Arab immigrants in the Detroit suburb of Dearborn that a mosque has been built. In the background is the huge Ford plant, River Rouge.*

tion is America's greatest treasure, and everyone can share in it. Why shouldn't we?"

The Middle East is geographically a part of Asia, but the cultural distinctiveness of the Arabs is such that they are seldom thought of as Asians. Like other Asians, however, Arabs have immigrated to the United States mainly for economic and political reasons. Their desire for educational opportunity has also been a strong motivating force.

Amal David, born a Palestinian, now a naturalized American citizen, is director of the bilingual program at Detroit's Southwestern High School. There are almost 200,000

*Amal David with her class of Palestinian students in Detroit*

Arabs living in the Detroit area, and Southwestern has a heavy Arab enrollment. Under Amal's direction the Arabic language is used along with English to make teaching most effective.

When Amal came to the United States in 1970 she was herself only a high school graduate. She was born in Nazareth in 1950, one of eight sisters. "When I finished high school," she says, "I looked around and saw that once my older sisters got married, that was the end of their educational careers. It would be the end for me if I stayed in Nazareth. I knew that. Being an Arab, I would have had a hard time getting into a local university.

"Since education is everything—Palestinians value education more than money—I decided to leave. I was able to get a student visa to study in the United States, but it took me two years to persuade my parents to let me come. They could not understand why I—a woman—would want to go to college. But at last they saw that I was determined to further my education, and I left with their blessings.

"I went to Lubbock Christian College in Texas. It was a strict, religious school, but that was all right. The terrible thing was the English. I thought I knew English well, but they do not speak it in Texas as they do in Nazareth. And I thought I would be disgraced if I did not make an A in every subject. In the end I did well, but I almost had a nervous breakdown. And I was so poor. I had to work to make ends meet. During the summers I sold Bibles door to door! You try that some time. It will help your English, and it will help you know Americans.

"I received a bachelor's degree in education at Lubbock Christian and then I was accepted for graduate work at Michigan State University. I earned a master's degree in communications there and then went to work on my doctorate at Ohio State University.

"Between degrees I returned to Nazareth. I am not sure whether I thought I would stay there or whether I meant it to be just a visit. But after I had been there only a short time, I knew I could not stay. I had changed too much. There you must be a conformist. You must be obedient, especially if you are an *Arab* and a *woman.* You must not question authority. I am proud to be an Arab, but it was difficult to be proud in Israel.

"My father and mother both saw how much I had changed. They both said to me, 'You must go back to America.' And now I am here to stay. I became a citizen just two months ago. I am so happy here. I can express myself politically without fear. I have a good job like this one at Southwestern High School. I can breathe.

"I have been talking about myself, but I might have been talking about tens of thousands of other modern Arab women. The role of Arab women is changing rapidly, not only outside the Middle East but in a number of Arab countries. Hundreds of women from my city, Nazareth, are today getting their education all over the world, many of them here in the United States as I did. And there are today thousands of Arab women who are doctors, lawyers, scientists, professors, managers.

"Did I say that education is everything? Well, perhaps it is not everything, but it is very, very important. It can open so many doors that would otherwise never be opened. That is what I tell my Arab students here in Detroit. Let education open a door for you."

# The Philippines:
# A Special Link with America

I F Y O U K N O W the Philippines, you sometimes wonder
why anyone would want to leave. When you first see that
country, whether your approach is by airplane or ship,
you are reminded of a lovely line from Joseph Conrad: "The
shallow sea that foams and murmurs on the shores of the
thousand islands, big and little. . . . ." There are over 7,000
islands in the Philippine Archipelago, 4,000 or perhaps more
so small that no one has bothered to name them; but each
island, big or little, has its own special beauty.

The great islands are Luzon, about the size of Illinois,
and Mindanao to the south, slightly larger than Indiana. On
these and the other large islands are volcanic mountains and
rain forests where fire orchids, bamboo orchids, and a thousand other species grow in profusion. The lowland plains are
dotted with emerald-green rice fields, and swift rivers run
down to the South China Sea and the Pacific Ocean.

The villages of fisher folk and farmers are friendly places,
as anyone who has visited them, especially at fiesta time,

knows well. The small cities are sleepy and relaxed, some with beautiful cathedrals, but the large cities—Cagayan de Oro, Cebu City, Zamboanga—pulsate with life. Manila, the capital of the Philippines, was long ago called the Pearl of the Pacific by appreciative travelers.

Yet Filipinos leave these islands every year by the tens of thousands to make new lives in the United States. Today the Philippines leads all other Asian nations in immigrants to the United States and stands second only to Mexico worldwide. Every year an estimated 6,000 Philippine nurses are recruited to work in American hospitals and most of them become permanent residents. Thousands of Filipino doctors practice medicine in the United States; over 4,000 of them through the years have come from just one school, the University of Santo Tomas in Manila.

Large numbers of other skilled and highly educated Filipinos are immigrating to America in a continuing flow: engineers, economists, agriculturists, business administrators. In many cases they bring wives and children with them. Many other Filipinos come to the United States under the immigration law that gives preference to persons who already have close relatives living in the country. In recent years Filipino immigrants to the United States have been in the range of 35,000 annually.

For all its beauty the Philippines is not a rich country, and lack of economic opportunity explains in part the movement of Filipinos to the United States. A Filipino nurse can make ten times or more in San Francisco what she can make in Manila. The difference for other occupations and professions can be even greater. Of course it costs more to live in the United States than in the Philippines, but the financial advantage of living in the United States is still great. It is a

common practice for many Filipinos living in America to reg-
ularly send money back to relatives in the Philippines.

But economics alone does not explain the large number
of Philippine immigrants to America, and it does not explain
at all the ease with which Filipinos move into American life
and culture. To understand fully the reasons why they immigrate and why they adapt so well, it is necessary to understand the very special relationship that has developed between the Philippines and the United States over the course
of the twentieth century.

The Philippines was under American rule from 1901 to
1946. When Commodore George Dewey sailed into Manila Bay
on May 1, 1898, Filipinos welcomed American help in their
fight to end more than three centuries of Spanish coloniza-
tion. The Filipinos, however, distinctly did not appreciate the
American decision to stay in the islands after the Spanish were
expelled. Bitter fighting took place between Filipino patriots
and American troops until 1902, when the better trained and
equipped U.S. Army prevailed.

The chief reason given for the American occupation was
a fear that some other country would take over the Philippines if the Americans left. Some U.S. politicians and newspaper editors of that time said that the Filipinos were not
ready to govern themselves. Historians today tend to agree
that, having moved from the Atlantic to the Pacific in their
own country, Americans were in an expansionist mood as the
twentieth century began.

Whatever the reasons, America and Americans were there
to stay for over four decades. Thousands of soldiers who came
to help the Filipinos and then to fight against them stayed on
to become businessmen, plantation owners, and traders. On
August 21, 1901, the military transport S.S. *Thomas* arrived in

Manila harbor with 540 American schoolteachers aboard. Thus began an era of educational development in the Philippines that continues to this day.

Education for Filipinos had been very restricted under Spanish rule, but now it blossomed. English became the language of instruction in all high schools, colleges, universities, and even in many private elementary schools. The deep-seated American belief in education as a stepping-stone to a better life took ready root in the Philippines. Today the country has a national system of higher education and a wide range of private colleges and universities, all patterned on U.S. higher education. Some of the largest universities in the world are in Manila; at least two have enrollments exceeding 50,000.

But despite powerful American influence in education, government, and business, Filipinos never wavered in their determination to gain political freedom. On July 4, 1946, after the bitter battles of World War II when Filipinos and Americans fought side by side against the Japanese, they achieved their ambition. The Stars and Stripes came down, and the tri-star and sunburst of the Philippine flag flew over an independent island nation.

The Philippines is and has always been strong in its own languages, culture, and traditions, but its links with America have stayed strong in the years since independence. English is still the language of instruction in the schools. The major newspapers are published in English, and it is the language used to bridge the numerous Philippine dialects. The Philippines has permitted the United States to maintain an important air force base and naval bases in the country. Millions of Filipinos know or have known one or more Americans at some time during their lives.

With this background it is hardly surprising that

*Horatio and Violeta Lotuaco and their daughter. Mr. and Mrs. Lotuaco are Filipino immigrants.*

hundreds of thousands of Filipinos have immigrated to America, and it is understandable that their adjustment to life in America is usually made with fewer problems than most immigrants encounter. Take the case of Horatio and Violeta Lotuaco, who grew up in the Philippines but now live in Bowie, Maryland, an attractive suburban town near Washington, D.C., Baltimore, and Annapolis.

Horatio was born and raised in Gapan, a town in the province of Nueva Ecija about seventy-five miles from Manila. His father was a dentist, his mother a teacher. Horatio went to school in Gapan and learned English there. When his father made trips to Manila, he would bring back American comic books as a special treat for his son.

"There were Philippine comics in the Tagalog language," Horatio remembers, "but I always preferred the excitement of American comics with Superman, Captain Marvel, and G-8 and his Battle Aces."

After he graduated from high school with top honors, Horatio went to Manila and enrolled at the University of Santo Tomas. He took a bachelor's degree in chemical engineering.

Violeta grew up in Manila, where her father was a civil servant. She went to a Catholic girls' school with high academic standards. After high school she too went to the University of Santo Tomas and took a degree in economics. Although they went to the same university, Violeta and Horatio did not know each other and in fact never met while they were living in the Philippines.

Horatio's chemical engineering degree enabled him to get a job as a technical aid at a sugar refinery in the provincial town of Tarlac. He worked there for a year but found both the job and the rural setting too confining. He moved back to Manila and took a job as technical sales representative with an industrial chemicals distributing company.

Horatio worked for the distributing company for four years. He did well, made good money and was given a personal car, a real status symbol then for a young man in Manila. But then the sense of dissatisfaction set in again. It was not the same as in Tarlac, for Manila had all the bright lights and excitement that a young bachelor could want. And yet in some ways the problem was the same, a problem of confinement that even now Horatio finds difficult to explain.

"The Philippines is a good growing ground for the young human spirit," he says, "but there comes a time when that spirit must put itself in an entirely new environment and test itself and experience new possibilities.

"I felt that I did not want to make a career of marketing bulk chemicals. There is certainly nothing wrong with selling and apparently I was good at it, but the excitement of the big sale was no longer there. Slowly the idea came to me of the excitement and possibilities of North America. I decided to apply to the U.S. Embassy in Manila for a permanent residency visa to the United States."

He did apply, and because of his training and experience as a chemical engineer, Horatio had no trouble getting an immigrant visa. Like many Filipinos who come to the United States, he already had a relative living there, a cousin in Virginia with whom he could stay until he found a job. Horatio began answering all newspaper advertisements for chemical engineers, and in three months he had found a job—working for a sugar refinery in Baltimore.

"You might think the wheel had come full circle," Horatio says with a laugh. "I started out working for a sugar factory in the Philippines and now I was working for one in America. But I assure you that working for a sugar refinery in Tarlac is not the same as working for a sugar refinery in

Baltimore. For one thing, you have more technical challenges and opportunities.

"It is true that living on my own in a big city in a foreign country was a trying experience. But I discovered new friends and new abilities. And there were the museums, art galleries, theaters, libraries! Altogether, I believe these experiences made me a better person."

For Violeta the process of coming to America was totally different. When she finished her degree at Santo Tomas, her parents gave her a trip around the world as a graduation present. She had every intention of returning to Manila and going back to school or getting a job, but when she reached Washington, D.C., her thoughts and her plans changed.

Violeta had an aunt and uncle who had lived in Washington for twenty years, and she visited them on her trip. As the visit stretched on, she found that she liked Washington, the people she met, and the general flow of life in America. And she felt comfortable, not at all like a stranger in a strange place. Before the month was out she had decided that she wanted to stay. She did not think then about whether she wanted to stay forever or just to work for a year or two and then return to Manila.

But to stay in Washington she had to have a job, and the problem was how to get one. Her wise aunt suggested that she try to find a job in an embassy. If an embassy wanted to hire her, the problem of securing a work permit would be solved.

There are well over a hundred embassies in Washington, and Violeta set out to visit them one by one. She does not remember now whether it was on the twentieth or thirtieth try, but finally, at the Bolivian Embassy, her patience was rewarded. They offered her a job as receptionist, and she took

*Violeta Lotuaco*

it. After a while, she left her aunt and uncle's house, rented her own apartment, and began to thoroughly enjoy the experience of being a young working woman in Washington. After a year she moved to a better job as information assistant at the Saudi Arabian Embassy.

And then she met Horatio. It was on a chance visit to Baltimore one afternoon, and she was simply accompanying a friend who was a member of an art workshop. Horatio had been participating in the workshop for some time, developing a deep-felt interest in art. He was there on the day of Violeta's visit, working on a large acrylic painting. It is not clear what Violeta thought of the abstract artwork, but it is clear that the two young people from the Philippines were attracted to each other.

Horatio began to make regular trips between Baltimore and Washington to see Violeta, and eight months later they were married. After some temporary apartment living, they bought their very pleasant four-bedroom colonial house in Bowie. By that time Horatio had moved on to a new job in Annapolis, and Bowie was an ideal location for both of them to commute to their jobs in Annapolis and Washington.

While he was working at the Baltimore sugar refinery, Horatio began a program of study for a master's degree in business administration at Loyola College. He got the degree and then transferred employment to the Anne Arundel County Public Schools where he now has a position as systems analyst. Horatio's work ranges from designing information systems that keep track of school property to systems that help teachers in student guidance. Developing management information systems gives Horatio a great sense of accomplishment and satisfaction that he never had in his previous positions.

Violeta too has moved on to new work. She is now an editorial assistant at the International Monetary Fund in Washington. It is work that lets her combine her economics background with the interest in informational publications that she has developed since coming to Washington. At sometime in the future she thinks she will go back to school for her master's degree.

A year after their marriage Violeta and Horatio made one

of their bedrooms into a nursery for their first child. Alessandra, whom they and everyone else call Alyssa, is now four years old.

In many ways Horatio and Violeta are like millions of young native-born American couples. They are successful, upward bound, ambitious for the future. They like their life in suburbia. They entertain friends, raise a vegetable garden every year, share the produce with neighbors, send Alyssa to summer camp.

There is no doubt that becoming Americans has been easier for Horatio and Violeta than it has been for millions of other immigrants. And yet, with all that, they know that they are special Americans, more than Americans in one sense. They are still close to their Philippine heritage, are proud of it, and like to share it with other Americans.

Although they have been completely bilingual in English for many years, Horatio and Violeta speak Tagalog, their native language, in their home. They made sure that Tagalog was the first language that Alyssa learned. When they took Alyssa to the Philippines recently for a visit, it was a great joy to everyone, especially her grandparents, to discover that she could speak the native language.

Horatio has become a naturalized American citizen. Violeta has not taken that step yet but thinks she will someday. "But," says Horatio, "it is not simply a piece of paper that makes you an American. Rather, it is a feeling of belonging and a deep conviction that you are one. If you have that feeling and that conviction, you are an American."

# III

NEW AMERICANS
FROM
LATIN AMERICA
AND
THE CARIBBEAN

*An immigrant Mexican family in El Paso*

M R. GONZALES and his "Anglo" business friend are relaxing in the spacious living room of Mr. Gonzales's Los Angeles home. Mr. Gonzales has just given his friend a delicious dinner of *pollo en mole verde;* they have finished their business and are now waiting for the Dodgers' game on television. Fernando Valenzuela is pitching tonight, and they are both loyal fans.

Mr. Gonzales manufactures a popular West Coast brand of canned Mexican foods, and he and his friend, a buyer for a grocery wholesale corporation, have just agreed on a large special order. Mr. Gonzales has been talking about the growing Latin-American population in the United States.

"There are 15 million Latin Americans living in the United States," Mr. Gonzales says in English, "perhaps many more. Living here permanently, I mean. In less than twenty years there may be 40 million. At least that is what the experts say. We have big families, you know, many children, many babies. And so many new people are coming every year from Mexico, Cuba, and Puerto Rico. More and more, too, from Central and South America.

"You know what that means for business. Young and growing families like Latin families buy many things. They buy food, clothes, cars, and furniture. They buy television sets, radios, tape recorders. They say 'Later we will save but now we need things'."

Mr. Gonzales's teenage son comes into the room and speaks to his father in Spanish. Mr. Gonzales takes a set of car keys from his pocket and hands them to his son. When the young man has gone, Mr. Gonzales's friend says, "Your son spoke fine English at the dinner table, but I see that when it comes to something important like borrowing the family car, he switches to Spanish."

Mr. Gonzales laughs. "You should hear his Spanish when he tries to convince me that he should have his own car. It is sheer poetry.

"And you know," Mr. Gonzales continues, "that brings me to the real point I wanted to make. Latin Americans are *hyphenated* Americans. I am a Mexican–American and so is my son. We have friends who are Cuban–Americans, Puerto Rican–Americans, and Bolivian–Americans. Do not misunderstand me. We have chosen to live in the United States, and we are Americans. Millions of us have become citizens, and our children born here are automatically citizens.

"But at the same time we take deep pride in our Hispanic heritage. Jet planes, telephones, and satellite communications make it easy for us to keep ties with the countries where we still have friends and relatives. And no matter what country we come from, we all speak the same language, except of course Brazil. So Spanish is very much alive in the United States. There are dozens of Spanish-language radio

stations, many Spanish-language newspapers, and some television stations. Latin-American music has become a part of
United States music, and Latin-American food is everywhere."

Mr. Gonzales's friend looks at his watch. "Latin-American baseball players are everywhere, too," he says with a
smile. "Concepcion, Andujar, Salazar, Trillo, Soto. But if you
don't turn on the TV you won't see Valenzuela tonight."

Mr. Gonzales rises and switches on the set. "I must see
every pitch," he says. "My father in Mexico City is a great
Dodger and Valenzuela fan. I must always call him after Fernando pitches and give him a complete report."

Mr. Gonzales is right about the size and importance of
Latin Americans, often referred to by the general term *Hispanics,* in the United States today. Because of immigration
and a high birth rate, their numbers are growing rapidly; by
the end of this century, they may surpass blacks as the largest
minority group in the country. Already they outnumber blacks
in such cities as New York, Los Angeles, and San Francisco.
One out of every five New Yorkers is Hispanic. Economically
the importance of the Hispanic population in the United States
is growing each year. At the present time it represents more
than 50 billion dollars annually in purchasing power. There
are thirty Hispanic-owned banks in the country and scores of
businesses that cater primarily to Latin Americans. And Hispanics have become an increasingly important force in American politics, especially in the states where the great majority
live: California, Arizona, New Mexico, Texas, Colorado, Illinois, Florida, New York, and New Jersey. Political parties and
politicians running for office are now very careful to reach
Hispanic voters and listen to what they are saying.

Because of their location in the Western Hemisphere, the

countries of Latin America and the Caribbean have always been considered important to the security of the United States. Because of this importance, special economic and military treaties have developed, as have programs of friendship and an "Alliance for Progress." The close geographic location is also responsible for the heavy flow of Latin-American and Caribbean immigration to the United States. The growing volume of this immigration has created problems, but in the long run it may bring about a greater degree of understanding and unity than treaties and government programs.

# The Pass to the North

**M**EXICO and the United States have a very special relationship. They share a 1,900-mile border. Their histories have been interwoven since the time of the Spanish conquistadores, and strong cultural and economic ties have developed between the two countries. The border states of California, Arizona, New Mexico, and Texas are heavily populated by persons of Mexican origin. In addition, millions of Mexicans enter those states and others every year—both legally and illegally—to visit relatives, vacation, shop, or work and return to their country. In recent years far more legal immigrants from Mexico enter the United States than from any other country.

El Paso, Texas, with a population of about half a million, is the largest city on the U.S.–Mexico border. El Paso's adjacent sister city Juarez, just across the border formed by the Rio Grande, is nearly as large at 400,000. El Paso is located in an ancient mountain pass, and its early name *El Paso del Norte* describes precisely what the city is: the pass to the north.

*Migrant workers—all from Mexico—harvest broccoli in the southern Rio Grande Valley.*

*Migrant workers in California*

Since its establishment in 1827, millions upon millions of Mexicans have poured through El Paso, many to remain permanently in the United States.

Three bridges connect El Paso and Juarez, and the flow of people over them continues twenty-four hours a day. The U.S. Immigration and Naturalization Service estimates that 36 million persons a year cross these bridges, at least 60 percent of them Mexicans. Of course, many of the same people cross the bridges every day. Thousands of Mexicans are legal U.S. aliens who work in El Paso but live in Juarez because it is cheaper or because their families are in Juarez.

At least 50,000 border-crossing cards are issued to Mexicans every year by the Immigration and Naturalization Service in El Paso. These cards entitle a person to visit the El Paso area for any legal reason except to hold a job. That requires a special work permit. Once a border-crossing card is issued, it is good indefinitely; there are hundreds of thousands of these cards in use at any one time. Holders of the cards can enter the United States for a seventy-two-hour period. Most cardholders come to visit relatives or to shop, and it is estimated that visitors from Mexico spend approximately $400 million in El Paso every year.

Human traffic over the El Paso bridges has a darker side. Every year thousands of criminal aliens—10,000 in 1981, for example—are stopped for trying to smuggle in drugs or other illegal materials (explosives, firearms) or for trying to avoid customs.

But for the overwhelming number of Mexicans who immigrate to the United States, one motive overrides all else: to find work that will lead to a better life. Such a motive brought Antonio Morales to El Paso in 1955, when, after a long wait, he had been admitted to the United States as a legal resident alien. Sitting in his modest but comfortable El Paso home one evening recently, Mr. Morales described his experiences as an immigrant.

"I was twenty-four," he remembers, "and I had a job. It paid—how do you say—peanuts, but it was better than anything I ever had in Mexico. I liked being a legal resident of the United States. I could walk down the street and wave to the Immigration Border Patrol.

"And then, after I had been in El Paso but three months, I was drafted into the U.S. Army! You can't believe it? Neither could I but it was true. You did not know that an alien

*Mexican immigrant farmer in the lower Rio Grande Valley*

could be drafted to serve in the U.S. Army? Neither did I, but, believe me, it is true. Three months a resident of the United States and in the Army!

"And yet it was not so bad. It was not bad at all, really. I had my basic training, and then on my first leave I returned to Juarez and married my fiancée, Vicenta. This was not long after the Korean War, you will remember, and I did not know where the army would send me. But I knew I wanted Vicenta to return to. Since I was in the army, she stayed in Juarez, of course.

"Well, do you know where the army sent me? Alaska! Fairbanks, Alaska! Imagine someone who has spent his whole life in the warmth of Mexico being sent to Alaska. I am three months living in the United States, and I spoke almost no English. Then I am in the U.S. Army, and then I am in Alaska! You ask if I would have come to live in El Paso if I had known all of this would happen? Oh, yes, I am sure of it. I wanted very much to work and live in America.

"And I told you, the army was not so bad. In fact, it was good in many ways, and it was good to see a new part of America, a faraway part like Alaska—not even a state then, you know. I made friends. There is my company picture on the table over there. I am in the second row. And I learned to speak English. It would have taken me much longer in El Paso. I think I served well in the army and I am proud of that.

"After two years I finished my army service and returned to El Paso. I got a job but it was not a very good one, so Vicenta and I and the children—babies were coming every year, it seemed—lived in Juarez where it was cheaper. Every day I crossed the bridge into El Paso to work and every night crossed back again.

"In 1961 I decided that we must live in the United States.

*Antonio Morales and his family in El Paso. Mrs. Morales has now been given legal U.S. resident status.*

I wanted my children to go to the good El Paso schools and to become American citizens. But you know what? When I applied to the INS—that is the U.S. Immigration and Naturalization Service—for permission to bring my family, I was told that I did not make enough money to support a family of that size in El Paso or anywhere in America. I was making $39 a week then. I know that is not much, but remember it was 1961 and money went much farther then. I thought we could live on that in El Paso, but the INS said no.

"So we still lived in Juarez and I still worked in El Paso. After some years, I cannot remember exactly when, I applied again to bring my family into the United States. I was working for a brick manufacturer then and making more money. But again the INS said no. They admitted that I was making more money, but they pointed out that I now had more children. My salary was still not big enough to take care of that size of family, they said.

"So that is the way it went. I was a legal resident of the United States and could live anywhere there I wanted to, but what good was that if I could not have my family with me? I tried other times but always the INS answer was the same. We stayed in Juarez.

"Now it was 1979, eighteen years since I first tried to bring my family to El Paso. Many of our children were grown and making their own lives in Mexico. But we had still five young ones at home and all of school age. They were also all American citizens. You ask how that is possible? It is simple. When delivery time came Vicenta would cross the border and have the baby in El Paso. Any person born in the United States is a citizen. Of course you know that.

"Then I discovered in that same year that I was eligible, because of my army service, to buy a house under the G.I. Bill. That is when I made the decision. I had some money saved and I had a job as maintenance mechanic with an agricultural products company. I bought this house, this one you are in tonight, and I brought my wife and children to live in El Paso.

"My children and I are here legally. My wife is not. But is that such a big crime? How can we stay here without wife and mother? If I can serve in the American army, if I can buy a house here, if I can hold a good job here, pay taxes and Social Security, why can we not live here as a family?

"We have applied once more for legal resident status for Vicenta. The Catholic Immigration Service is helping us, and I think this time the approval will come. All of our children speak English now and are doing well in school. One of our sons is a fine baseball player on the Little League team. See the trophy there on the table? They like it in El Paso. They are going to be good Americans. We are all going to be good Americans. I applied for U.S. citizenship three months ago. It is late but not too late, I think."

# The Undocumented

HEADQUARTERS for the United States Immigration and Naturalization Service (everybody calls it the INS) Border Patrol is an attractive cinder block building near the El Paso airport. Behind the headquarters building is the INS Processing Center, which is actually a detention center for persons suspected of entering the country illegally. In this center is a courtroom where three immigration judges hold hearings and decide cases of illegal entry. Ninety percent or more of all persons in the Processing Center are Mexicans, but one hears the expression OTM's, which stands for Other Than Mexicans because aliens of other nationalities do cross the U.S.–Mexican border illegally: Salvadoreans, Guatamalans, even Europeans now and then.

Also behind the Border Patrol headquarters is a compound which at any given time may contain fifty to one hundred cars, trucks, minibuses, pickups, and station wagons. These are vehicles that the Border Patrol has seized from smugglers of human beings. Smuggling illegal aliens from El

*Undocumented immigrants, rounded up in Operation Jobs, are detained by the INS in El Paso shortly before being sent across Mexican border.*

Paso and other border points to other U.S. cities is a big business. In 1982 undercover immigration agents smashed a smuggling ring that was transporting about 25,000 illegal aliens a year, mostly Mexicans, to cities in California, Colorado, Illinois, Indiana, Kansas, Michigan, Missouri, New Jersey, New York, Wisconsin, and Wyoming. Almost 16,000 illegal aliens were transported to Chicago in the course of a year! The ring was said to be grossing $24 million a year, of which as much as $15 million was profit.

The Border Patrol is constantly on the lookout for "coyotes," as these smugglers of human beings are called by Patrol personnel. They have learned that beneath a load of firewood in a pickup truck half a dozen illegal aliens may be hiding. A horse trailer may be full of aliens, even if there is a horse in it. An innocent-looking car may have a false back seat hiding as many as three aliens.

"Sure, we catch 'em," says one Border Patrolman, "a lot of them. We confiscate their vehicles and sell them at public auction. But if you're a coyote smuggling 200 or 300 aliens a month and averaging maybe $500 profit on each one, you've got plenty of money to buy a new car whenever you need one."

Smuggling is a felony, and smugglers are often fined or put in jail. But the financial rewards are great, and, just as in drug smuggling, there are the moguls, the big money men, who have coyotes working for them and almost never get caught themselves.

Who are these illegal aliens who pour across the border in a never-ending nighttime flood? Nine out of ten are wretchedly poor men, and some women, from all over Mexico who could never qualify as regular legal immigrants. They are called "undocumented" aliens by the INS because they do not have immigration papers or a "green card"—a work permit which entitles a legal resident alien to hold a job in the United States.

Most of these illegal aliens have practically no money and will try to get away from the border by walking or riding freight trains. Some will stay in border cities and towns or try to get jobs on nearby ranches and farms. Others do have some

*Senior Border Patrol Agent Mike Calvert walks the Texas-Mexican border near El Paso.*

money because they have saved for years or sold everything they own or have relatives in the United States who will pay the smugglers. Those are the ones who go to the coyotes for help.

At about four o'clock in the afternoon Senior Border Patrol Agent H. M. "Mike" Calvert leaves Border Patrol headquarters in an unmarked car headed for the sand hills west of El Paso, where the Texas, New Mexico, and Mexico borders all come together. This lonely stretch of semidesert is Mike's patrol territory, and it is a favorite border-crossing area for illegals.

Today Mike has a visitor with him, a journalist writing a story about illegal aliens. The journalist is in El Paso for a look at the border situation, so Mike drives first to the Rio Grande which flows down from New Mexico and forms the Texas–Mexican border all the way from El Paso to the Gulf Coast.

On the way to the river Mike sees two men looking in a large trash bin behind a store. "I think they're illegals," he says to his visitor and brings the car quickly to a stop. He gets out and says politely in English, "Gentlemen, can we talk for a minute?"

The two men whirl around and stare at Mike. They are young, dark-complexioned, not badly dressed. They say nothing. "What is your citizenship?" Mike asks, still speaking English.

The men continue to stare at him. They clearly do not understand what he is saying. Mike switches to Spanish, and after a moment the men smile, looking a bit embarrassed, and answer him in Spanish. The three of them talk a bit longer, and then Mike activates the car radio and says, "Three-o-three. I have two." He gives the location and asks, "Can someone pick them up?" The radio crackles and a voice says, "Five minutes."

The two illegals stand beside the car. They are silent, but they do not seem upset. The journalist, still inside the car, is wide-eyed. "How did you know they were illegals?" he asks Mike.

"You develop a sixth sense when you've been in this business as long as I have," Mike says. "That's twelve years. It's a lot of little things, hard to explain. Their not understanding English was an indication, though there are a lot of legal resident Mexican aliens here who can't speak a word of it."

"How long have these two been in El Paso?" the journalist asks.

"About an hour," Mike says. "They just crossed the river and walked here. They told me they were going to try to catch a freight train to Houston tonight. The freight yard is just a few blocks from here."

A Border Patrol car drives up. The two Mexicans, after being searched for weapons, climb into the back seat, and the car drives away.

"What will happen to them now?" the journalist asks.

"They'll be taken to the INS processing center at the main bridge," Mike says. "A record will be made of their illegal entry, and they'll walk across the bridge back to Juarez. They may wait until dark and cross the river again. With a little luck they might still catch that freight to Houston tonight."

The journalist seems astonished. "I don't understand this at all," he says.

They drive to a residential part of El Paso and within a few minutes are on the U.S. bank of the Rio Grande. "That's Mexico right on the other side," Mike says.

The journalist climbs out of the car, and now there is a look of real bewilderment on his face. *"That* is the *Rio Grande?"* he asks.

At this point and as far as the eye can see in both directions, the river seems not more than fifty feet bank to bank. The water can be no more than knee deep.

"Why," the journalist exclaims, "you could roll up your pantlegs and wade across in twenty seconds."

"And thousands do every month," Mike tells him. "Farther downstream toward Laredo the river is much wider, much more water. You have to take a boat or swim across. That's where the term 'wetback' came from."

They get back into the car and drive up the river road toward the center of El Paso. While they are still in the residential area, they begin to see small groups of men and a few women sitting on the Mexican bank of the river. "They're waiting for dark," Mike says. "Then they'll come across. The Border Patrol has fifty seconds or maybe a minute to catch them after they reach the U.S. side. After that they've faded into a neighborhood or into the city or they make it to a house where they wait for coyotes to pick them up. They know where those houses are located."

The journalist asks, "Do people who live in these neighborhoods ever call the Border Patrol and report illegals?"

Mike is silent a minute then he says, "No. But their dogs bark. That's about the only help we get."

Now they arrive at a chain link fence, perhaps eight feet tall, that runs along the U.S. bank of the river. "This fence was put up a few years ago," Mike says. "It's three or four miles long, I don't know exactly. Then they stopped building it. People said it looked too unfriendly—like the Berlin wall."

"Does it help any?" the journalist asks.

*A Mexican waits for a moment at a hole in a border fence.*

Mike smiles. "People call it the Tortilla Curtain," he says. "They say it's thin and flexible and the Mexicans eat it up. They do too." Mike points to a hole that has been cut in the steel fence. "There are a dozen or more holes like that along the fence. We used to patch up a hole when we found it, but there would be another cut someplace else the next night. Now we leave them and actually the fence does help a little or at least the holes do. We watch the holes the best we can and stop more of them that way."

As the sun sinks toward the mountain called Cristo Rey which towers over El Paso, they see increasing numbers of people waiting on the riverbank. Some have already waded across the river and are looking through the fence on the U.S. side.

"It would take an army to stop everyone," the journalist says.

"A big army," Mike agrees, "on duty twenty-four hours a day. There are just six Border Patrol units in this whole area."

"Then what's the use?" the journalist asks. "Even the few you catch can come right back."

"We catch a lot, not a few," Mike says. "If there was no Border Patrol at all, I think you would have people coming over the border like a wave of locusts, not just Mexicans but Salvadoreans, Guatamalans and just about everyone else. I'm sure thousands of people never try it because they know there are Border Patrol agents. And some that get caught don't try it a second time."

"Of course, you're right," the journalist agrees. "But what about jail? Crossing the border without going through immigration is against the law. If you put them in jail, wouldn't that stop it?"

"We put the coyotes in jail," Mike says, "and sometimes illegal aliens if they get in trouble or have an extensive arrest record. But if every one we caught was put in jail, you'd have to have a jail as big as El Paso and an army of jailers and 500 judges. Even if the country could afford it, that's not the answer."

"No, it isn't," the journalist agrees. "But what is the answer?"

"If anyone knows, I haven't heard it," Mike says. "But there is one thing that might help. If a fine could be levied against every illegal alien caught and if the money could be used by the Immigration Service to pursue illegal aliens, we'd catch a lot more, a whole lot more."

As they drive on, Mike speaks again. "There's something else. Ninety-five out of a hundred of these illegals aren't bad people. They just want one thing—to get a job, work hard, and send money home to help their poor families. If they could make a decent living in Mexico, there wouldn't be any illegal alien problem, at least not much of one."

By now they have driven out of El Paso and are climbing into the sand hills. There are no paved roads here, and the land seems desolate and lonely in the rapidly gathering darkness. The hills that stretch south into Mexico are dotted with scrub brush. A chill is in the evening air.

"The ones who cross the border here instead of at the river are doing it the hard way," Mike says. "But if they get past us here, they have a lot better chance of making it on into the country. It's mostly Mexicans from the provinces who come through this way. They don't like the big cities."

Mike stops the car, gets out, and walks up one of the many faint trails that wander through the brush. The journalist follows him, pulling his coat a little tighter against the night chill.

"How do you ever catch anyone out here?" he asks.

"We've learned to do what the Indians used to do," Mike tells him. "We cut sign. If I see a cigarette butt or an empty tomato can or a candy wrapper, I start looking. This sand holds footprints real well, and I look for those."

He shines his flashlight along the trail and picks up a faint shoe print. He bends over and examines it. "That one's old. You learn to tell the difference. And we have sensors buried in these trails. If someone steps on one, a signal goes off at headquarters and I get a radio message.

"We've learned these trails and can usually circle around in the car and get ahead of a person or a group. If we miss, we can call in a helicopter when it gets light. And of course all of the highways around here have Border Patrol check-points."

The journalist is still staring at the shoe print. "It's like a game of cat and mouse, isn't it?" he says.

Mike snaps off the flashlight. "Well, I guess so," he says. "But it probably doesn't seem like much of a game to a man who has walked for three weeks to get here."

ILLEGAL ALIENS are probably the most serious immigration problem facing the United States today. The sheer numbers are bewildering and disturbing. Precise figures are impossible to obtain for the simple reason that persons living in the United States illegally do not want to be counted. Informed estimates suggest that from 3 to 6 *million* illegal aliens may be living in the United States. Some estimates go as high as 10 million, and a former Commissioner of the U.S. Immigration and Naturalization Service says that the figure could be 12 million! Estimates of the number of new illegal aliens coming into the United States annually with the intention of staying indefinitely range from 100,000 to 500,000.

The concentration of illegal aliens in certain urban locations causes special problems. An INS estimate in 1976 showed that the illegal alien population of both New York City and Los Angeles might be close to 1.5 million. Houston was estimated to have half a million illegal aliens. Cities having from 400,000 to 200,000 were Chicago, Miami, San Antonio, Newark, San Francisco, and San Diego. Such high concentrations of illegal aliens can cause severe problems of housing, education, unemployment, welfare, and other social services.

One clear fact about illegal aliens is that the great majority come from Mexico. Of over one million deportable aliens located in 1976, 93 percent were Mexicans. The others were from all over the world, with relatively large numbers of students from Africa and Asia who had come to the United States as college students and had simply not returned after their visas expired.

Another clear fact is that the number of illegal aliens coming into the United States is increasing. In 1970 about 350,000 illegals were apprehended by the INS. The number apprehended increased in every year but one until 1979 when it totaled more than a million. More effective apprehension by the INS may have accounted for some of this increase, but the basic reasons are to be found in a rapidly growing population in Mexico plus a sluggish national economy and fiscal policies that have benefited the wealthier classes and left millions in dire poverty.

Dr. Leon Bouvier, Director of Demographic Research and Policy Analysis of the Population Reference Bureau, wrote in 1979: "Today, Mexico's rate of economic growth is a mere 2 percent annually while its population growth rate is at least 3.2 percent. Therein lie many of the root problems which precipitate massive moves across the border—both legal and illegal." Bouvier points out that, if Mexico's current growth rate continues, its present population of 64 million will double in a little over twenty years.

According to Mexican writer Irma Salinas Rocha, "The poor are much poorer now than they were during the revolution of 1910." And she asks, "Is this progress?"

What can be done about the millions of illegal aliens now living in the United States? How can millions more be kept from entering the country? These questions remain unanswered. Some special interest groups argue that illegal aliens play a useful role in the United States, doing work that sufficient numbers of American citizens can no longer be found to do: such work as cutting sugarcane in Florida, building fences on Texas ranches, picking apples in Virginia, harvesting sugar beets in Colorado, picking and ginning cotton in southern New Mexico, doing low-level factory jobs, and cleaning and other service work in restaurants and motels all over the country. Some business owners maintain that they could not survive without this pool of relatively low-paid labor.

On the other hand, American labor unions believe that illegal aliens, large numbers of refugees, and high levels of legal immigration pose a threat to American workers and are one cause of increasing unemployment of American citizens. Studies on this subject have produced conflicting findings. Some have indicated that illegal aliens are not a serious problem in taking jobs that Americans want. Other studies seem to show that illegals are filling some jobs that would be attractive to American workers.

Pressure is growing in the United States to do something about illegal immigration, but policymakers and other concerned persons cannot agree on what to do. At this time only one thing seems certain. To quote a former Commissioner of the Immigration and Naturalization Service, "The problem is mind-boggling."

# The Haitians

T
HE NEARBY Caribbean country of Haiti is one of the
poorest in the world. Eighty-five percent of the country's population of 6 million lives below the World
Bank's absolute poverty level figure of $135 per year. Unem-
ployment is a disaster. Over half of the working-age residents
of the capital city of Port-au-Prince are out of work. Much of
the population lives in a constant state of hunger and malnutrition. One child out of every five dies before the age of
four. Haiti's food production is declining by 2.5 percent every
year.

The Haitian government, headed by "President for Life"
Jean-Claude (Baby Doc) Duvalier, has not been effective in
fighting these problems. "Haitian government corruption and
insensitivity to the plight of the average Haitian are perva-
sive," says a recent House Foreign Affairs Committee staff
report.

Haitians have been coming to the United States for a long
time, both legally and illegally, but until recently their num-

*In Miami the Golden Door is a halfway house for Haitian and Cuban refugees. Here, a VISTA volunteer with a Haitian girl.*

ber was relatively small. Then in 1980 and 1981 they began to arrive by the tens of thousands. They did not try to go through immigration procedures, for they knew that would take years or, more likely, they would never be allowed to come.

So they came by small boats, traveling the Windward Passage between Cuba and Haiti. The boats were often old, leaky fishing vessels. Some broke up in stormy seas and all aboard were drowned. Bodies washed up on the beaches of south Florida. But thousands of Haitians reached those shores alive and disappeared into the countryside or into the shelter of the "Little Haiti" section of Miami. Many were caught by immigration authorities almost as soon as they climbed out of their boats and were put into federal detention centers.

Why did these Haitians, mostly men but some women also, make the perilous sea voyage to risk detention and an unknown future in a strange land? Here are some of their stories.

MARCEL, *32, working as a day laborer in the grapefruit orchards of Immokalee, Florida.*

"Why did I leave Haiti? I will tell you, but first, Sir, I must ask: have you heard of Ton-Ton Macoutes? No? Well, we have a saying in Haiti, 'Do not curse the crocodile's children while you are still in the water.' But now I am out of the water, out of Haiti, that is, and I will tell you about Ton-Ton Macoutes. They are the volunteer police or army of President Duvalier. I do not know exactly how to describe them, but they have the power, and they are every place in Haiti. Like the crocodile's children, they are the children of Duvalier, not his children in blood but in evil deed.

"I was a fisherman in Haiti, a poor fisherman, but I could catch some fish every day. I would keep one or two and trade or sell a few, and that way I could put barely enough food in the mouths of my wife and six children and keep a poor roof over our heads.

"And then one day when I was bringing in my catch, two Ton-Ton Macoutes from my village came to me and said they wanted fish. I asked how much they would pay. They just laughed and took two of my best fish and walked away. I knew what the Ton-Ton Macoutes could do if you opposed them so I said nothing. That night there was not enough food for my family.

"The very next day the same two Ton-Ton Macoutes came

again and asked for fish. Perhaps I should be ashamed, but I was afraid, and I let them take two. Before I had even reached the market, two more Ton-Ton Macoutes stopped me and asked for fish. I had already made up my mind what I would do if that happened. I had picked up a heavy stick from the roadside, and I held it in my hand like a club.

" 'You can have fish,' I told them, 'but you must pay for them.'

"The Ton-Ton Macoutes looked at my stick, and one of them said, 'Are you threatening us?'

" 'I am not threatening you,' I told them, 'but you cannot take my fish unless you give me a fair price for them.'

"These Ton-Ton Macoutes did not have guns as some do, and it is known that I am a strong man. 'You will be sorry,' one of them said, but they turned their backs and walked away.

"That night a friend came running to my house and said to me, 'You must go away quickly and hide. The Ton-Ton Macoutes are coming to arrest you. They say you have threatened them and they are going to put you in jail.'

"Everyone in Haiti knows what happens when you are put in jail by the Ton-Ton Macoutes. You may be beaten, even killed or kept there until your family buys your freedom. My family has no money, so I ran away as my friend said I should.

"The Ton-Ton Macoutes looked for me, but I hid with different friends. And I sent word to my wife to borrow money from the moneylender because I must escape to America. If I went anyplace in Haiti, I would have no boat and could not make a living. Besides, the Ton-Ton Macoutes are everywhere.

"My wife borrowed the $500 needed for my passage, and

I found a boat that was making the trip soon. Thank God the sea was quiet and we reached Florida with no trouble. Thanks to God also I was not caught and put in a detention camp. Now I make $25 a day. I do not work every day of course, but most days I do, and I send almost all of the money to my wife.

"She does not receive all of it—there are many sticky fingers in Haiti—but most of it she gets. She is repaying the moneylender—the interest is so great—and our children have more food and clothes than they have ever had.

"I miss my wife and my children. I miss the sea. I am a fisherman, not a fruit picker. It may be that I will stay here forever. I do not know. Perhaps someday my wife and children can come to live in the United States. Perhaps someday it will be safe for me to return to Haiti. In Haiti we have another saying, 'There is a cure for everything except death.' We are all alive and I can hope."

RAYMOND, *40, day laborer on a vegetable farm, Delray, Florida, living in a workers' barracks*

"No, I was not afraid of Ton-Ton Macoutes. Why should I have been? I had nothing to steal, only hungry mouths to feed—a wife and twelve children. We have a small piece of land in Haiti, but the soil is poor, there is no money for fertilizer, and every year there seems less food for the table. Sometimes I worked in banana plantations and on road repair, but the money I earned was very little. Three of our children died or there would have been fifteen. When the last one died—she was but two years old—I said to my wife, 'I must go to America,' and she bowed her head and said, 'I know.'

"So I borrowed passage money from the moneylender. I

said, 'I will send money to pay you back.' He smiled and said, 'I am not worried.' What he meant was that if I did not pay back the loan and the interest, he would take my land, and then my wife and children would truly starve.

"And so I am here in Florida, and I am sending money back, and my wife has written me that our children are healthier than they have ever been. I pray every day that an immigration officer will not come and take me to a detention center. I have no green card, no permit to work. But I must work or my children will die.

"People have told me that if the immigration puts me in a detention center, I must say that I am a refugee. I tell them I do not know what is a refugee. They say a refugee is someone who fled from his country because he was afraid the government would kill him or put him in prison because they do not like the way he thinks. I do not know about things like that. I left my country because if I did not come here my children would starve, and my government did not care whether they starved or not. I am a refugee from hunger."

COLETTE, 21, who, with her husband Claude, is being held as an illegal alien in a federal detention center.

"My husband, Claude, and I were caught by the immigration as soon as we waded ashore and we were brought to this place called Camp Krome. We have been here six months, but there are others who have been here more than a year. There are too many people here. It is too crowded and there is nothing to do all day long except sit and think. We are not mistreated, but it is terrible to do nothing. And the men and women are separated, so I cannot see my husband except for a few minutes now and then.

"Why did we come to America? Claude and I were born

in Port-au-Prince and grew up there. We went to school for a few years, but our families were poor and we had to stop. We were married when I was seventeen and he was eighteen. Claude has never had a real job in his life. There is nothing for a young man to do in Port-au-Prince.

"My grandmother gave me some gold jewelry when I was married. It was all she had in the world but she wanted me to have it. I sold it and it gave us just enough money to buy passage to America. And what do we have to show for the little bit of gold we had? Six months in prison. The immigration tells us we can go back to Haiti any time we want to. They will send us back. Claude says we should go. He says he cannot stand being here in Krome any longer. But I tell him if we go we will have wasted our gold, and we will never have any more gold in Haiti. We will be worse off than when we left.

"Maybe they will send us back anyway. But I know that if we say we do not want to go, the immigration cannot send us back until an immigration judge has heard our story. He will decide whether we can stay or whether we must go. But why does it take so long for the judge to hear our story?"

WITH ONLY a change of details the stories of Marcel, Raymond, and Colette could be the stories of most Haitians who have landed on the shores of Florida in the last few years. They have all been driven from Haiti by fear, poverty, the hope of a better life or all three motives. For some time, the U.S. government made very little effort to detain them; but as their numbers increased, the Immigration and Naturalization Service was instructed to put new arrivals in detention centers and start deportation proceedings against them.

Under United States law, any person who comes into the

(*Above and following pages*) *Haitian refugees in Florida*

country, no matter how or why he comes in, is entitled to a hearing before an immigration judge to decide whether he should be allowed to stay or whether he should be deported. With the help of civil rights lawyers, almost all of the Haitians in detention have said that they want deportation hearings, and they have maintained that they should be allowed to stay in the United States because they are refugees.

Over 2,000 Haitians were detained for months, some for

*A Haitian refugee is learning English in Miami.*

more than a year, awaiting hearings. The problem was that there are not many immigration judges, and besides that, volunteer lawyers needed time to prepare the Haitians' cases. Strong efforts were made by civil rights groups to have the Haitians released until the time of their hearings. These groups pointed out that alleged illegal aliens of no other nationality—Mexicans, Cubans, Salvadoreans—had ever been detained as a group for such a long period.

The U.S. government pointed out that the flow of Haitians to the country had almost stopped since the detentions had started. The government said that if the Haitians were released, it would be a signal for thousands more to come. Some sources said that over 40,000 Haitians had already left Haiti and were waiting in the Bahamas to come to the United States if it became clear that they would not be placed in detention centers for a long period. Finally, in July, 1982, a federal court decided that the Haitians in detention must be released until their hearings were held.

This humane decision was welcomed by many people, but it did not answer the question of whether the Haitians are refugees. There were even more serious questions that it did not answer. How many refugees can the United States take? Which refugees, of all those in the world, should be given preference for coming to this country?

# The Cubans

W HEN FIDEL CASTRO came to power in Cuba on New Year's Day, 1959, the United States was affected in many ways. There was now a Marxist-Socialist country with close Russian ties on the U.S. doorstep. And as a result of the new Communist-oriented government, the first wave of refugees from a Latin-American country reached U.S. shores.

The destination of most of those fleeing Cuba was south Florida, and from 1959 into the early sixties they arrived by the thousands. Many of these new arrivals were upper- and middle-class professional people—doctors, lawyers, college professors, bankers, business managers—who had opposed the dictator Fulgencio Batista as well as Castro who replaced him. Although most of them arrived penniless, they had the education, experience, and determination to succeed.

And succeed they did. By the 1980s the Cubans were a well-established and important part of Miami and south Florida life. An impressive number of Cuban doctors and lawyers

*Cubans relax in a small park in Miami.*

are in practice. There are almost 3,000 Cuban-owned businesses, which include construction companies, restaurants, boat companies, and shoe, clothing, and cigar factories. Miami has Cuban-owned or controlled banks. The chairman of the Capital Bank in Miami is an immigrant from Cuba. Financial experts have called the bank "stunningly successful."

Miami has a Spanish-language newspaper, *Diario Las Americas,* and a number of Spanish-language television and radio stations. The highest-rated radio station in the Miami area broadcasts entirely in Spanish. As a result of the strong Cuban and Spanish language influence in Miami, the city has become a major shopping center for Latin America, with tourists coming from all over South and Central America. It is estimated that Latin American tourists spend $1.5 billion annually in Miami and south Florida.

While a large number of Cubans fled from their country after Castro gained power, the refugee flow to Miami and south Florida took place over a number of years. This time frame made their assimilation into the life of the area relatively smooth. But in 1980 came a human deluge from Cuba that caused great problems in south Florida and severely tested the Immigration and Naturalization Service and the volunteer agencies that they asked to help them.

It began on March 28, 1980, when a busload of Cubans crashed through the gate of the Peruvian embassy in Havana and asked for political asylum. This dramatic incident triggered a rush by thousands more Havanans to the Peruvian embassy. They stormed into the embassy compound and asked for asylum. They also asked for safe passage out of Cuba to some other country.

At that point President Jimmy Carter announced that the United States would welcome some of these Cubans as political refugees if the Cuban government would let them leave the country. He did not say how many the United States would take. Castro was apparently angered by Carter's statements and also saw an opportunity to get rid of a great number of dissatisfied people, some of whom were making trouble for him. He decided to create a problem for Carter and the United States by letting a large number of people leave the country. During the six months between March and Oc-

*This Cuban refugee in Miami was a boat person.*

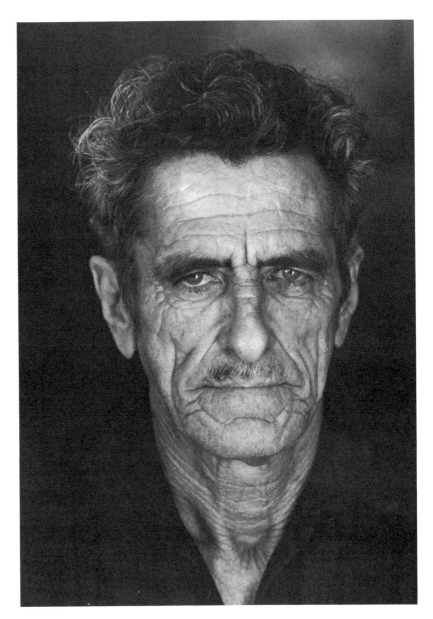

*Cuban refugee in Miami*

tober of 1980 over 120,000 Cubans departed from the port of Mariel in a boatlift that became known as the Freedom Flotilla. The people in the boatlift were called "Marielitos."

The destination of all of these small boats was the same: the south coast of Florida. As this new wave of Cubans landed on the Florida shores, they were picked up by the INS. Whenever possible they were put in touch with relatives already living in the United States. In most cases Florida state and volunteer agency officials helped find them a place to live and processed their papers for emergency financial help.

Very quickly a disturbing discovery was made. In addition to the tens of thousands of persons who had fled in the Mariel boatlift because they wanted to leave Cuba, the Cuban government had taken thousands of prisoners from Havana and other jails and forced them into boats to the United States. Others were taken from mental hospitals and put aboard the boats. In all, 22,000 Marielitos admitted to the INS that they were convicts, taken from Cuban prisons and forced to come to the United States. Many other Cuban convicts slipped through the INS screening process by denying that they had any criminal background. Proving otherwise was very difficult for the INS.

The Cuban government's flooding of south Florida with refugees and the particularly heartless action of forcing convicts and mentally disturbed people into the Mariel boatlift has sometimes been called "Castro's revenge." There is no doubt that Miami and other south Florida communities were hard hit by this totally unexpected flood of people. Social services in these cities were pushed to the limit and beyond. Volunteer agencies such as the Catholic Refugee Resettlement Program, Lutheran Social Ministries, and Church World Service staggered under the loads assigned them.

Crime rose alarmingly in south Florida after the arrival of the Marielitos. In 1981 Miami was in first place on the FBI's annual list of the most crime-ridden cities. Two other south Florida cities were in the top ten. Marielito criminals were thought to be responsible for half of the violent crime in Miami.

Yet in the end, Castro has not had any revenge. The American people, the U.S. government, and many state and city governments have proved equal to dealing with the crisis of the Mariel boatlift. Over 60,000 of the Marielitos have been settled in south Florida. The others have been placed with sponsors in other parts of the United States.

The criminal elements have been dealt with effectively. Several hundred who committed crimes after arriving in the United States, some of them serious crimes, have been caught, tried, and imprisoned. Intensive interviewing of the 22,000 who admitted a criminal record in Cuba revealed that many of them were political prisoners and that others had been put in jail for avoiding military service or stealing food. Careful placement with sponsors has made it possible to release most of these. About 1,500 who could be classified as serious criminals are still being held in federal prisons. A few hundred mentally or emotionally disturbed Marielitos are also still being held.

When looked at in the context of the more than 120,000 Mariel boat people who arrived in 1980, the number of those who have not been successfully resettled is very small. As *The Washington Post* said in an editorial early in 1982: "Fidel Castro undoubtedly thought he would embarrass and discredit our government by unloading his undesirables on the beach at Key West. He must be disappointed. Americans have accorded the migrants both charity and justice."

One problem for the Cubans who came in the Mariel boatlift is that they have all suffered in the public eye from the backgrounds and criminal acts of a relatively small number. Even the well-established Cubans who came to Miami and south Florida in the 1960s have tended not to be very sympathetic to the newcomers because of the problems and bad image they have created. They feel that after twenty years under a socialist government, the Marielitos can't adjust to a free society where success is based on ambition and hard work.

But time is proving that it is wrong to apply such stereotypes to the Mariel boat people. Thousands of them left Cuba because they could no longer stand the political and economic straitjackets they were in. They are demonstrating that they know how to work hard and make progress in a democracy.

Take the case of Augustin, a young man who worked hard but got nowhere under Castro's brand of socialism. He was not one of those that Castro wanted to get rid of, but when the Mariel boatlift began, he made up his mind that, whatever the cost, he would leave Cuba. Augustin tells the story of what happened.

"Bueno. I am lucky to be here, you know, lucky to be alive. The boat I was on was no good. It was overloaded, and it listed to starboard almost from the time we left Mariel. When we were near the Florida coast, the boat broke. I was thrown into the sea, but I was saved. I have told you that before.

"You ask why I fled from Cuba? Bueno, I will tell you. I was a boy, maybe ten or eleven, when Castro came to power. My father was a master plumber, but he knew about politics. He said to me, 'Life will be different now. Very hard. Just learn to work and be quiet. Do not do anything or say anything to make government people notice you.'

"My father taught me to be a plumber, and I was good at that work. Before I was twenty, I was a plumber helping to build government ships, and I learned engine repair also. I always had more work than I could do. The shipyards needed me.

"I made money. Oh, yes. There is no doubt of that. But what can you buy in Cuba? What can you spend money on? There is no way for young people to enjoy life in Cuba, no dancing, no good times. I felt like I was suffocating. Always I felt that way.

"I forgot what my father had told me. With a group of other young men, I began to do things against Castro's government. Not things like bombing or hurting people. We made posters making fun of the socialist government, criticizing Castro and the way he was running Cuba. And we were caught one night when we were making posters. We were called Enemies of the People.

"I think I would have died in prison, but remember, now I was a master ship's plumber and a skilled engine mechanic, and the government needed me very much. So I was allowed to go on with my work, but I was watched closely and I knew it. Now I was suffocating more than ever.

"Then came Mariel. I saw people going to get on boats, sailing out to a freedom I longed for and had never known. The government said that anybody who was not happy in Cuba could go in the Mariel boatlift, but that was not true at all. When I said I wanted to go, my supervisors laughed at me and told me to go back to my work. I was needed in Cuba, they said.

"But I had made up my mind that I would leave Cuba, even if I died in trying. One day instead of going to work at the shipyard, I went to the government office where people

*Augustin, a Cuban refugee*

had to be approved to go in the Mariel boatlift. There was a huge crowd there. People were shouting, 'Let us go or kill us!' I joined the shouting and the crowd and we all pushed into the building. Somehow in the confusion my papers were stamped. I was free to go. It was a miracle maybe bigger than the miracle of being saved after my boat sank.

"Bueno. I reached the United States, and after a while I was sent to Fort Chaffee in Arkansas with many other Marielitos. Finally, after three months, I had a sponsor and was let out. You know the rest. I have been in Oklahoma City for almost two years now, working in a good hotel. At first I was put in housekeeping because they did not know what I could do. Now I am in maintenance working on plumbing and machine repairs.

"I am happy here. I have friends. I am free to buy things, to have a good time. I work hard, and it is good to work hard when there is a reason to do so. I think there are many, many Marielitos like me."

# Who Are Refugees?
# How Many Can
# the United States Take?

T HE UNITED STATES has always been a haven for persons being persecuted because of their religious or political beliefs. The Pilgrims, who made America their home in 1620, were the first refugees to reach these shores. Since that time, untold thousands have come to this country to escape tyranny and to be free to live according to their beliefs.

In more recent times immigration law has limited refugee status to persons fleeing from Communist-bloc countries and from the Palestinian-Israeli conflict. In 1980, however, Congress passed a law which defined a refugee as a person "who is unable or unwilling . . . to return to his country because of persecution or a well-founded fear of persecution on account of race, religion, nationality, membership in a particular social group, or political opinion." Under this law, politically or religiously persecuted people anywhere in the world can ask for refugee status in the United States.

As a young and growing nation, a giant in size, blessed

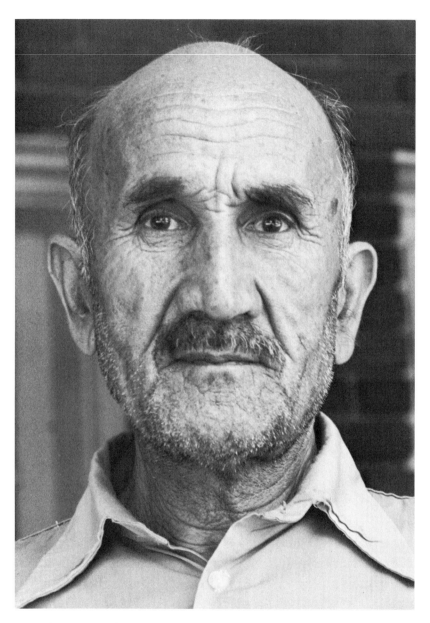

*An Afghan grandfather in Oklahoma City*

*An Afghan refugee teaching children*

with a dazzling abundance of natural resources, the United States seemed able to welcome an almost unlimited number of immigrants, whether they were fleeing political or religious oppression or whether they simply wanted to make a better life for themselves. That perception began to change early in the twentieth century, and now, as the century reaches its final decades, Americans are increasingly aware that their country is no longer underpopulated and that its resources are far from unlimited.

At the same time, it is clear that the world of today is

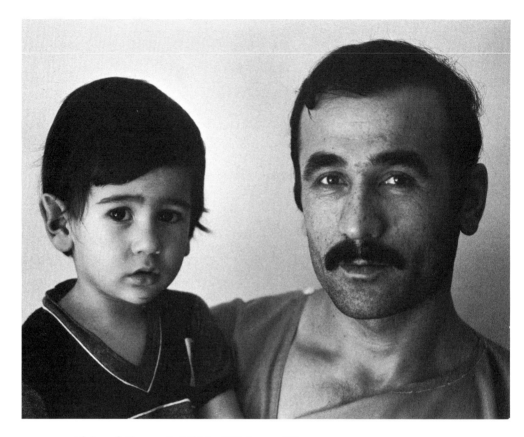

*Afghan father and child in Oklahoma City*

one of increasing political and economic turmoil. The number of refugees in the world at the present time is estimated at between 8 and 13 million. Over 2 million Afghans have fled their country in the wake of Russian support for the government in power and are living in Pakistan. As many as 5 million Africans are living outside their countries as refugees to escape ancient tribal hatreds. Hundreds of thousands of Indochinese still remain in refugee camps, and large numbers of Palestinians continue to live as refugees.

How many of the world's refugees can the United States

*Afghan grandmother and granddaughter in Oklahoma City*

take for permanent settlement? Congress pondered that question, and the 1980 law specifies that the number of refugees entering the United States in any one year will be limited to 50,000. However, the law allows the President to admit an unlimited additional number of refugees if he believes it is necessary to do so. The President's only obligation is to advise and consult Congress if he increases the refugee limit. In 1981, just a year after the 50,000 limit was imposed, over 200,000 refugees were admitted to the country.

Even with presidential latitude, the 1980 law does call for restraint. The flow of refugees from distant parts of the world can be reasonably well controlled, since it would be almost impossible for them to reach the United States without help from the U.S. government. But people from nearby countries such as El Salvador, Cuba, and Haiti are quite a different matter. They can and do enter the United States by way of Mexico or by making a short sea voyage. The INS estimates that half a million Salvadoreans may now be illegally in the United States.

How many Salvadoreans, Guatamalans, Nicaraguans, Cubans, and Haitians are here because they are politically persecuted? How many have come because of the poverty in their countries? If people from nearby countries pour into the United States in such large numbers, how can room be made for immigrants and refugees from the rest of the world?

Even with the most liberal immigration and refugee policies, the United States can take but a small percentage of the people worldwide who are desperate to come to this country. Distinguishing between true refugees—people who face persecution or even death because of their political or religious beliefs—and those who are trying to escape wretched poverty is both painful and difficult today and is likely to become more so in the future.

# The Golden Handshake

A s MIGHT BE expected in a great world capital, Washington, D.C., has attracted large communities from widely different parts of the globe. Its Chinatown in the downtown area is old and well established. The concentration of Vietnamese in the northern Virginia suburbs is one of the largest in the country; there are over 500 listings of the name Nguyen in the phone book. Salvadoreans have arrived in large numbers since the troubles of the early 1980s in Central America, and refugees from European countries have always found Washington a welcome haven.

For almost twenty years a steadily growing number of West Indians have made Washington their home, mostly Jamaican but also immigrants from Barbadoes, Guyana, Tobago, Trinidad and some of the smaller Caribbean island countries. In the early 1960s only a few hundred West Indians lived in Washington, but an increase began in 1965 when immigration entry quotas were raised for the Caribbean countries that had only recently gained their independence.

Previously their quotas had been restricted because of

their colonial ties to European countries. The West Indians enthusiastically welcomed their increased quotas and immediately began to take advantage of what they called "the Golden Handshake." Today over 10,000 West Indians live in Washington, and their number is growing.

The West Indians have concentrated in a heavily populated downtown area, but they have not formed a ghetto. They are well intermingled with large numbers of American blacks, whites, and Latin Americans. The West Indians have gained a reputation for being hard working and ambitious, and they have a particular fondness for starting their own small businesses. Reggae music pours out of half a dozen West Indian record shops day and night, and from Jamaican cafes and bakeries drift the delicious smells of coconut turnovers, meat pies, and curried chicken and goat, always served with rice and brown beans.

"We grow up with the idea that America is a magic place," says one West Indian businessman. "When we get here we find out that what we believed is true, but you have to make the magic happen yourself, through hard work."

One of the most interesting and most successful of the thousands of West Indians who have come to Washington since the year of the Golden Handshake is Keith Fagon. Keith is a Jamaican, tall and splendidly built. He wears his hair in the matted Rastafarian style, although he is not a member of that unusual Jamaican religious cult that believes the former and now dead Emperor Haile Selassie of Ethiopia is the reincarnation of God. Keith came to Washington as a college student in 1969. Today he is a publisher and editor of a high-quality, highly successful magazine published on Capitol Hill, *The Hill Rag*.

Keith graduated with top honors in science from Clarendon College in Jamaica and could have had a scholarship for graduate study in England. "But I wanted to come to America," Keith says. "I had an older brother in Washington, and I couldn't wait to get here. My brother was deep into the American black movement and ideas of negritude, and I wanted to get into those things too. Thinking about them just set me on fire."

Keith enrolled in courses in black studies at the Federal City College in Washington. He went to seminars on the black movement, attended special lectures, read literature. He kept at it for a year or more, and then he pulled away. "I didn't need it," he says. "If other people got strength from it, that's fine, but it wasn't for me. There were a lot of other things I wanted to think about."

Keith received a scholarship from the English Department of Johns Hopkins University in nearby Baltimore and took a master's degree in creative writing. "But do you know where I got my real education?" Keith asks. "From the Library of Congress. I was living on the Hill, and I found out you could just walk into the Library of Congress and read books. I read books on philosophy, geography, psychology, sociology, every subject under the sun. It's the greatest library in the world, and I was there every day for over three years. I read all day and then I drove a taxi at night to make enough money to live on. I must have slept sometimes, but I don't remember when."

And then a store owner friend of Keith's, Jules Gordon, gave him the idea of starting a newspaper that would be primarily an advertising medium for merchants in the Capitol Hill area. The paper would be given away free, and the cost of putting it out would come from selling advertising space. "I didn't know anything about newspapers or advertising," says Keith, "but I knew about words and ideas, and I thought it might work into something worth doing."

With the help of Tawny Harding, a friend who became a partner and part owner, the first issue of *The Hill Discount Rag* was published late in 1976. It was little more than an advertising flyer, printed on yellow legal-sized paper. The word "discount" was used because the paper contained coupons that could be clipped and presented to the advertiser for a discount on the item purchased. "Discount" was later dropped, and the paper became *The Hill Rag.* Keith and Tawny distributed the first issue with the help of a few neighborhood kids.

The first and hardest problem was selling advertising. Merchants were skeptical. They didn't think the paper would last. Similar efforts had been tried on Capitol Hill in the past and had folded after a few issues. They were very doubtful about distribution. They had heard about young people being paid to distribute papers but instead throwing them down sewers and into trash bins.

The job of selling advertising space fell mainly to Keith. Keith has an easy, friendly, persuasive manner and a smooth flow of words packaged in a delightful Jamaican accent. "Keith could be one of the world's greatest salesmen," says a friend. "You've heard about the guy who sells refrigerators to the Eskimos? Well, Keith could sell them snow."

Selling snow to Eskimos, Keith found, might be easier than selling advertising space to Hill merchants in what most of them thought of as a fly-by-night venture which would soon collapse. But he kept at it. Visiting the same merchants over and over, writing sample ads for them, and sometimes as a last resort, offering a free spot for one issue. He sold twenty ads for the first issue, twenty-two for the second. It was slow going but it was a start.

*Keith Fagon, a newspaper editor from Jamaica, in his Washington, D.C. office*

It would take many things to make *The Hill Rag* a good magazine, Keith knew, but there was one thing that would spell quick disaster, and that was poor distribution. He went to work on that. The only practical way to distribute the paper to houses, apartments, and Senate and House of Representative offices on Capitol Hill was door-to-door delivery by neighborhood boys and girls.

There were plenty of youngsters who wanted the part-time work. The task was to find the good ones and win their confidence and friendship so that they would want to do a good job. Keith worked side-by-side with them in getting the papers ready. He talked with them, fed them, played ball with them, visited their homes. The effort paid off. *The Hill Rag* distribution system far surpassed anything like it that had ever been seen on Capitol Hill. Other business people with material to distribute door-to-door tried to get Keith and his crew to do it for them.

Advertising space became easier to sell. The paper got bigger and better and went to a regular tabloid format. Except for taking out barely enough money to live on, Keith put everything back into the paper, buying photographic and layout equipment and paying for better printing.

Then came the work that Keith was really interested in: making *The Hill Rag* a real Capitol Hill community magazine and not just an advertising handout. He added news stories and feature stories about people and events on Capitol Hill, a thorough calendar of Washington activities, business briefs, even short essays and an occasional short story appropriate to the paper's readers.

After seven years *The Hill Rag* is still growing and improving and today can accurately be called a magazine. There is a staff of ten now. The focus is still on Capitol Hill, but advertising is received from businesses all over Washington, and the paper is distributed in many places besides the Hill. Journalism departments of a number of universities send student interns to do summer work on *The Hill Rag* as part of their training.

Keith is proud of what he has accomplished, but he says quite bluntly, "This never could have happened in Jamaica. There is no way a person can start there with nothing but an idea and build it into what I have here. I think the United States is the best place in the world for going as far as you're good enough to go. And it doesn't make any difference whether you're black, white, brown, yellow, or green, for that matter."

There is absolutely no doubt that Keith Fagon feels America has given him the Golden Handshake.

# I V

---

## NEW AMERICANS
### FROM
### AFRICA
### AND EUROPE

---

*Ethiopian refugee in Dallas, Texas*

THE MINISTER-COUNSELLOR stood up from his desk, motioned his visitor to a chair beside the coffee table, and sat down on a couch opposite him. He poured coffee for both of them and then relaxed. The visitor had made an appointment to talk about immigration, and the Minister-Counsellor had a good deal to say. He had been a diplomat for twenty years in the service of his West African country and had been stationed in the United States for a number of those years.

"What I have to say is about Africa below the Sahara, of course, black Africa," the Minister-Counsellor said and added for emphasis, "the ancestral home of every black American today. It has always seemed to me that there are several ironies about the immigration of black Africans to the United States.

"The first irony is that there has been so little of it after the forced immigration of the slave trade. Of course one can understand why Africans would not have wanted to come here during the nineteenth century, even after the Civil War. The memories of slavery were still too fresh. America was no land of opportunity for black people then.

"But at this time in the twentieth century, it is quite different. There are certainly Africans who would like to immigrate to America, not as many as you might think perhaps, but a good number. But now, at a time when hundreds of thousands of Asians and Latin Americans are immigrating to this country, only the tiniest trickle of immigrants is coming from black Africa. Definitely less than 3 percent of the total immigration to the United States each year.

"And why are there so few immigrants from Africa? It is because of your immigration policies. First preference in selecting immigrants is given to people who have close relatives in the United States. Family unification it is called. But if very few immigrants have come from Africa since the slave trade, then of course very few Africans today have close relatives here. There are millions of blacks here with the same roots as the Africans who want to immigrate but no brothers, sisters, parents, or children. So Africans cannot qualify under family unification.

"The second reason for immigrant selection is job skill. If you are an engineer, a doctor, a nurse, you have a good chance to be approved for immigration to the United States. Most of the immigrants from Africa to America today are people with these high skills. And that is the second irony about African immigration. The Africans that the United States is willing to accept as immigrants are the very people that African countries can least afford to part with. All African countries today desperately need highly trained people—doctors, nurses, economists, engineers, teachers. They get their education, sometimes abroad, and then they leave Africa. Not many, but still too many because we have so few. We call it the brain drain, you know, and it is a serious problem.

"And the third reason the United States may accept a person for immigration is if he or she is a refugee. Here again I see an irony, perhaps the biggest of all. Africa has more refugees than any other continent, maybe 5 or 6 million. No one really knows. But the United States takes only a small handful of African refugees while it takes countless thousands of people fleeing from European, Southeast Asian, and Latin-American countries.

"Do you know why? Until very recently by U.S. definition a refugee was someone fleeing from a Communist country. Otherwise, he couldn't be a refugee. It was as simple as that. Since there were no Communist countries in black Africa, there were no refugees.

"But it wasn't that simple, of course. Some of the most desperate political refugees in the world are in Africa. Perhaps you know the history but let me tell you anyway. In the last century, European countries divided black Africa among themselves as colonies. They drew the lines for countries according to agreements among themselves. It made no difference to them if a country contained two or even more tribes that had been deadly enemies for centuries. It made no difference to them if a large tribe was split between two countries. But when the African countries gained their independence in this century, these completely artificial national lines were fixed. So you had enemy tribes fighting each other for political power. You had tribes in different countries wanting to be united. The result has been bloody internal wars—and refugees by the millions. But American officials do not understand these things.

"Now just one more thing. It seems to me that there will

never be many immigrants from Africa as long as the three criteria of family unification, job skills, and refugees are applied. I believe—and I know that many American blacks believe—that it would be a good thing if the number of African immigrants was a little more in line with the numbers that come from Asia and Latin America.

"Why could a certain number of immigrants not be accepted for the old reason, the original reason, that brought most immigrants to this country: simply to try to build a better life for themselves? I am sure some means of selection could be found, and then more Africans could come.

"A final point. I don't think there would ever be a flood of immigrants from Africa even if immigration regulations permitted. Many might come for a short time, but they would go back. Family ties among Africans are the most binding force in life. Even if people go away, in the long run they come home if they possibly can. It is the way our culture works. Even after death they want their bodies sent home— to Africa."

THE COUNTRY of Ethiopia probably is Africa's most disturbing example of disastrous numbers of refugees caused by confining people with different traditions, religions, and ethnic backgrounds within national boundaries created long ago by European colonial powers. Ethnic Somalis have roamed the Ogaden area of Ethiopia since time immemorial. In the last few years over a million of these nomadic herders have sought refuge in the neighboring country of Somalia, where their ancestral tribal ties have always been. They have been driven there by a war between Ethiopia and Somalia over the Ogaden, and now they live miserable lives in refugee camps.

In the northernmost part of Ethiopia is the province of

Eritrea, which borders on the Red Sea and the country of Sudan. The people of Eritrea are different by language and tradition from the ruling Amharas of the central highlands of Ethiopia. Eritrean nationalists have fought for more than twenty years to try to gain the province's independence from Ethiopia. This conflict has driven into exile large numbers of people who were either fleeing the Ethiopian army or who did not want to be drawn into the struggle between the freedom fighters and the government. Most of these people, half a million or more by some estimates, have sought refuge in Sudan, but some have made their way to Egypt, Italy, Germany, and the United States.

Refugee status for Ethiopians was made possible in the eyes of U.S. immigration authorities in 1974 when a Marxist military regime was created after the overthrow of Emperor Haile Selassie. This new regime was aided by Russia and also by Cuba, which sent 12,000 or more troops to fight against the Somalis and the Eritreans.

Far outnumbering the Ethiopian exiles who have managed to reach the United States are thousands of Ethiopian students who were studying in U.S. colleges and universities when the Marxist government took power. Some 15,000 of these students have asked the U.S. government for refugee status since they do not want to go back to a Marxist, Russian-backed country. They have been allowed to stay in the United States, but a final decision has not been made as to whether they will be allowed to stay permanently in the country.

Dallas, Texas, has been the resettlement city for several hundred Ethiopians who fled the country and were given refugee status by the U.S. government. Few are Somalis from the Ogaden because almost all of them have chosen to stay in

(*Above and following pages*) *Ethiopian refugees in Dallas, Texas*

the Somalia refugee camps. Many of the refugees in Dallas are Ethiopians who are opposed to the Communist-oriented government or who have reason to fear it because they worked for the old government. Many are Eritrean liberation fighters who were hunted by the government. There is no middle ground today for many Eritreans. They are under pressure to be loyal to the Ethiopian government on one side and to help the liberation forces on the other. They must choose or flee the country. Hagos is one of the Eritrean refugees now living in Dallas. Like a good many of these refugees, Hagos has a good education. He was enrolled at Haile Selassie University

in Addis Ababa studying economics when the Marxist government came to power.

"I was still enrolled at the University," says Hagos, "but
actually I was in the town of Asossa teaching at the high
school. In Ethiopia all university students must teach or do
other work for a year between their junior and senior years.
This is really a good idea because Ethiopia needs educated
teachers. This national service plan had been part of Haile
Selassie's government for a long time.

"But when the Marxists took over the government, they
started a major campaign against students. They were afraid
of students because that is where political trouble starts in
Ethiopia—in the universities and high schools. The government took 60,000 students out of the high schools and universities and sent them out into the villages to teach the peas-
ants. At least that is why they said they were taking them out
of the schools. Really it was to scatter them to the winds so
they would not make trouble.

"My future did not look good at all. I am Eritrean, you
know. I did not think the new government would let me go
back to the University. And they would probably try to keep
me from returning to Eritrea. They might keep me teaching
school in provincial towns and villages for years. Or who
knows? They might decide I was dangerous and arrest me.

"Two other Eritrean University students were teaching
at the Asossa school. They had the same doubts and fears as
I, and when the rainy season came, we decided that we would
leave Ethiopia. There is an army base in Asossa, but we were
not worried about that. At that time of year the rain comes
down in torrents. If you are out in it, you think you will
drown. The roads turn to rivers of mud, and soldiers do not
come out of the base unless they absolutely have to. So one

night we simply walked across the border into Sudan. Our only problem was to keep from sinking in the mud.

"We made our way to a small town and reported to the police. We told them we were refugees from Ethiopia, and they passed us on to a bigger town called Kassala. Already so many refugees had been coming from Ethiopia that the United Nations High Commission for Refugees had established a field office in Kassala. We were processed quickly and sent to Khartoum, the capital city of Sudan.

"There I was very lucky. I had my University record, my transcript, with me, so the United Nations gave me a scholarship and I was accepted at Khartoum University. I finished my degree in economics there.

"After that I was given a visa to go to Germany, and I stayed there for two years. I worked at the reception desk of a good hotel. Since I knew English well—all high school and university education in Ethiopia is in English, you know—it was not hard to get a good hotel job like that in Germany. There are so many tourists who speak English.

"I wanted to go back to a university and work for a master's degree, so I studied German. But after two years, I knew that I would not be able to do graduate work in German for a long time, so I decided to try to come to the United States. Again I was lucky because by now the United States had decided that Ethiopians escaping from the Marxist government being helped by Russia and Cuba could be considered refugees.

"And so I was given a visa to come to the United States, and the Dallas Catholic Charities arranged for me to come here to Dallas. Now I am working in their Refugee Resettlement Program helping other Ethiopians to settle here. I am enrolled in a university night program studying for a master's in labor and industrial relations.

"I think about becoming a U.S. citizen. I also think about going back to Eritrea. The Ethiopian government says we are welcome to come back, that they would be happy to have us back. But I think if I went back I would be arrested. If I go back, I think I will have to slip in, just as I slipped out.

"Did I tell you? The two friends I left Ethiopia with have gone back. They have slipped back into Eritrea to join the liberation forces. One of them went to Khartoum University like I did. The other went to London and became a Ph.D., in engineering I think but I am not sure. And then they went back to Eritrea. Many Eritreans who have left have gone back just that way. They have become doctors, engineers, nurses and then they have gone back to fight for the freedom of Eritrea. But I do not know what I will do."

The story of Hagos, a refugee from Eritrea, is very different from that of Dr. Carl Alexander Reindorf, a man who was born and raised in Africa but who now makes Washington, D.C., his home. At first glance Dr. Reindorf might seem to be the worst example possible of the "brain drain" that the Minister-Counsellor was talking about. In reality nothing could be further from the truth.

Carl Reindorf was born and spent much of his early life in Accra, the capital city of the West African country of Ghana. His mother was a midwife, a woman who assists other women in childbirth. This type of medical worker is very important in Africa. Carl can remember his mother coming home from delivering a baby and sometimes saying, "That was a sickle."

Carl knew that his mother was talking about an inherited blood condition that can cause a disease known as sickle cell anemia. But he could not have dreamed then that the day would come when he would be a leading research specialist on this strange and painful disease that afflicts black people almost exclusively.

From an early age, however, Carl did have a sense that someday he would be a doctor. Not only was his mother a midwife, his father was a "dispenser" or pharmacist who worked in government hospitals. In time his father became chief dispenser and began to move from hospital to hospital throughout Ghana. His family moved with him, and Carl got to know about hospitals all over the country.

Carl also had a great uncle, Charles Elias Reindorf, who was the third Ghanian ever to become a medical doctor. During the course of his career Carl's uncle became the leading authority in West Africa on treating yaws, a tropical disease that can destroy a person's skin and bones.

"With a background like that," Carl Reindorf says, "it would have been strange if I had become anything but a doctor." And he adds with very American slang, "I had medicine coming out of both ears."

After secondary school, Carl studied science at the University of Ghana. There were no medical schools in Ghana in 1952, so after finishing at the University of Ghana, Carl went to England and enrolled at London University. He took his medical degree there and then began twelve years of intensive study and practice in pediatrics, the branch of medicine that deals with the health and diseases of children.

Dr. Reindorf's work took him to a number of countries, principally the United States, Canada, and back to Great Britain, but during that long period he did not return to Ghana to practice medicine. Among many positions, he was Pediatric Resident both at Jacobi Hospital in New York City and the Hospital for Sick Children, Toronto, Canada. He was also a Fellow in Pediatric Hematology at the Hospital for Sick Children. Hematology is the study of blood and blood-forming organs.

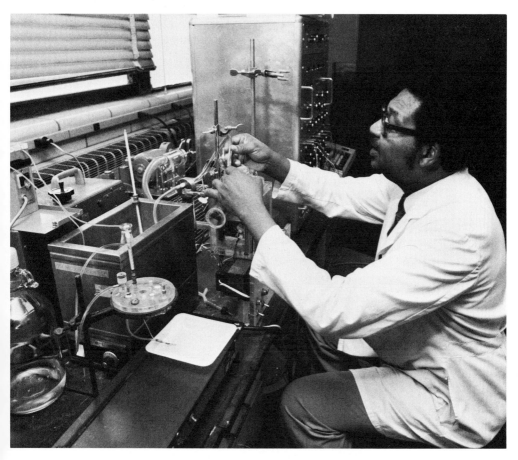

*Dr. Carl Reindorf in his Howard University laboratory*

Dr. Reindorf was Director of Pediatrics at Sydenham Hospital in New York City and also Director of the Sickle Cell Clinic there. He is particularly proud of the fact that the City of New York gave him an Award for Distinguished and Exceptional Public Service. The award was given for four years of work in giving medical help to poor and homeless sick people in Harlem.

But then, in 1969, Dr. Reindorf decided that it was time to return to Ghana. Sickle cell anemia was commanding more and more of his time and thought, and he wanted to work with it in Africa, where, in the distant reaches of history, it had had its beginning.

Sickle cell anemia takes its name from the fact that in some people, predominantly of the black race, some abnormal red blood cells develop a sickle shape instead of the normal round or disc shape. As the sickle-shaped cells increase in number, they do not flow smoothly through the veins. The result is an anemic condition, clogged veins, and an insufficient blood supply to many organs of the body, the central nervous system, and the long bones.

Persons with sickle cell anemia suffer times of great pain in their arms, legs, and abdomen. They have increased susceptibility to certain diseases such as pneumonia and meningitis. They may also be retarded in their physical growth.

Sickle cell anemia is inherited. Many millions of black people in Africa and America carry the sickle cell trait but suffer no ill effects from it. Sickle cell anemia itself occurs only if *both* parents carry the sickle cell trait. In that case, there is a 25 percent chance that any child born to them will have sickle cell anemia. Although much has been learned about treating sickle cell anemia and lessening the suffering of its victims, there is at present no cure for the disease.

When Dr. Reindorf returned to Ghana in 1969 he threw himself into work on sickle cell disease. He became Senior Lecturer in the Department of Child Health at the Ghana Medical School. At the same time he became Pediatrician-in-Charge of Newborn Services at the Korle Bu Teaching Hospital in Accra and in addition was Director of the Pediatric Sickle Cell Disease Clinic at the same hospital. His work and research led to a series of papers on sickle cell disease in Africa, which he presented at major international scientific meetings.

In 1976 Dr. Reindorf made a crucial decision. With seven years of work on sickle cell anemia now behind him in Africa, he became convinced that he could best continue his research in the United States. "In Africa," he explains, "the study of sickle cell anemia can be complicated by many other conditions: malnutrition, malaria, typhoid and other fevers, measles. In the United States sickle cell disease is likely to be found in as pure a state as it can be found. I thought I was ready for that. I thought I could learn more."

Dr. Reindorf returned to the United States and took a position as Clinical Associate Professor of Pediatrics and Child Health at Howard University in Washington, D.C. Howard University is one of the world's leading centers in sickle cell anemia research, including research in alleviating symptoms of the disease and making its victims more comfortable.

Dr. Reindorf's speciality is rheology, a science dealing with the flow of blood. He is working at Howard University on the use of blood substitutes in treating sickle cell anemia sufferers. He is still in the data-collecting stage of his research and knows that the results he seeks may be years in coming. "It is tedious work," he says, "but rewarding, too. I will keep on. That is why I am here."

Although Dr. Reindorf is eligible to apply for American citizenship, he has not made up his mind about taking that step. "But," he says, "America is the land of great opportunity for all peoples on this earth who want to use their talents for the betterment of all mankind."

One thing Dr. Reindorf is sure of is that the work he is doing on sickle cell anemia will benefit Africa as much as it will America. In addition, Dr. Reindorf has helped to found the Association of African Physicians in North America and is chairperson of its board of directors. The Association already has about a hundred members, all African doctors studying or working in America. The purpose of the Association is to bring them together in a number of ways to attack the health problems of Africa.

"For years people have rightly been concerned about the brain drain from Africa," Dr. Reindorf said recently. "From the Association of African Physicians in North America we will have enough trickles from the drain to form a pool. And from the pool we will help to irrigate the medical deserts of Africa."

IN THE PAST, Europe was the great source of immigrants to America. Today the immigrant flow from that continent has pinched off to a small percentage of what it was in the nineteenth and twentieth centuries. In fifty years the number of immigrants from Europe has dropped from 80 percent to 13 percent. Why?

The reasons are to be found in the changes that have taken place both in Europe and the United States during that time. Many of the countries of western and northern Europe, and to some extent those of southern Europe, have experienced substantial development and prosperity since World War II. There are more employment and educational opportunities in Europe now, hence less reason for people to immigrate. Also, population growth in many European countries has slowed down or stopped altogether in recent decades. Stable populations have made the "teeming masses" of Europe a thing of history.

At the same time America is not seen so much as the

land of opportunity that it once was. Its own population has grown to 232 million. Unemployment has been a serious problem during some periods, and labor unions and government regulations have placed restrictions on certain kinds of jobs. Opening a business, even a small one, may now require a substantial amount of money. Free or very cheap land is largely a thing of the past.

All of these factors, both from the European and U.S. sides, have led more and more Europeans to the conclusion that they are better off, or at least as well off, staying where they are.

Another reason for the decline in immigration from Europe is that the Soviet Union and other Communist-bloc countries discourage their citizens from leaving permanently and in many cases refuse outright to let them go. In earlier years millions of immigrants to the United States came from some of these countries, particularly the Soviet Union and Hungary.

The problems of Jews who wish to leave the Soviet Union are particularly disturbing. Although the Soviet government has allowed about 250,000 Jews to immigrate to other countries since 1971, over 2.5 million Jews still live in the Soviet Union. At present almost one Jew out of five in the world lives there.

Officially sponsored anti-Semitism, discrimination against Jews, has been growing in the Soviet Union for a number of years. This discrimination takes many forms: interference with Jewish religious and cultural practices, fewer career and educational opportunities, even physical abuse and jailing of some Jews. Discrimination and harassment of this type have led increasingly large numbers of Soviet Jews to seek to leave the country.

*Russian Jewish immigrants study English in New York City.*

Applying for permission to leave the Soviet Union is a frightening and dangerous step for a Jew. Often he is fired from his job or demoted to a lesser position. Pressure is put on his relatives to make him change his mind. The application may take months or even years to work its way through the bureaucracy, and there is never any guarantee that the application will be approved. Finally, a Soviet Jew must renounce his citizenship when he applies for permission to emigrate.

"There is no turning back," said one Jewish emigrant from the Soviet Union. "We must make it in whatever country we go to. We can never go back to Russia, even if we wanted to."

Most Jews who leave the Soviet Union immigrate to Israel, but a good many go to the United States. Over 16,000 have resettled in the greater New York City area in the past ten years, and Jewish communities in other cities throughout the United States have helped other thousands to become established.

"To immigrate is not just to cross an ocean," said one Jewish immigrant to America. "It is to enter a whole new world. And here in this world, in America, I am free to be a real Jew. My children can hold up their heads and be proud of their Jewish origin."

One serious problem is that the Soviet government ties emigration to international politics. When relations are fairly good between the Soviet Union and the United States, the Soviets let more Jews leave the country than when there is tension between the two countries. In the latter years of the 1970s about 30,000 Soviet Jews were allowed to emigrate each year. By the early 1980s the number had pinched off to a trickle of 2,000 or 3,000 a year.

This sharp decline resulted from bad U.S.-Soviet relations brought on by the Soviet invasion of Afghanistan, the breakdown in arms limitation talks, and Russian fury at the U.S. withdrawal from the Moscow Olympics. The situation regarding Jewish emigration from the Soviet Union may change again if conditions improve between the two countries. But at the present time the prospects are bleak. An official of the National Conference on Soviet Jewry said recently, "This is undoubtedly the worst of times. We're talking about the end of emigration."

Refugees and in some cases regular immigrants from the Communist-bloc countries are not limited to Jews, of course. During the past thirty years every case of political crisis in a country involving an intensifying of Soviet control has re-sulted in an increase in refugees. This has been true of Hun-gary, Romania, Czechoslovakia, and Poland. Many of these refugees stay in other European countries, but a certain num-ber make their way to the United States.

The case of Vladimir Najdrovsky and his family is typical in certain ways of many European refugees. The Najdrovskys are now beginning new lives in a midwestern U.S. city, but until a few months ago they had spent their entire lives in Czechoslovakia. Their home was in the capital city of Prague, where Vladimir was a graphic artist, and his wife Iva was an architect. Bohumil, their twelve-year-old son, and their daughter Gabriela, eight years old, were enrolled in good schools.

But life was not easy in Czechoslovakia for Vladimir. "Even though I was born and raised in a country which was governed by a Communist regime, I could not and cannot bring myself to believe in the Communist ideals," he ex-plains. "I was pushed many times to join the party but I never did, even though I knew that if I was a party member I would have benefits that I did not have. It was later shown to me that I could not even keep my job because I was not a party member. I was only allowed to do manual labor."

Vladimir, who is a commercial artist by trade, talks can-didly about his troubles. "In 1968 when the Russians came into Czechoslovakia, I did not hide my feelings and spoke openly about the disaster which fell on my country. It was bad enough before the Russians invaded, and it was becom-ing worse day by day. Many people pretended and did not express their feelings openly but I just could not bring myself to do this, and as a consequence in 1969, I was taken in for investigation.

"I was asked about my beliefs. I thought that it was all over after that one time, but I was wrong. Many times over the years since then I have been taken in for interrogation. I was not put to trial in 1969, but suddenly in 1980 I was called to trial. Twelve years later I was put before a court without any proof of guilt."

Vladimir managed to get his trial postponed, and then he knew that somehow he and his family were going to have to try to escape from the country. Already he and his wife had been informed that their children could no longer go to the schools they were attending. Iva was still allowed to work as an architect because her skills were needed in remodeling buildings in Prague, but how much longer she would be able to keep her job was very much in doubt.

For an entire family to escape from a Communist country is extremely difficult, and Vladimir knew that any possibility of success lay in deceiving the Czech government officials in charge of foreign travel. He began by convincing a doctor that their daughter Gabriela was sick and needed to spend some time in a warmer climate. With the doctor's certificate, he applied for permission to take the entire family to the Mediterranean island of Cyprus for a vacation.

The trip was approved, but Vladimir had to pay all expenses of the trip in advance and was allowed to take no money from the country. They could take nothing but clothing, and the police made a careful inspection of their home to make sure that was the case. When they finally flew out of Prague, they left behind every worldly possession—home, furniture, money in the bank, everything. They had only the clothes in their suitcases.

As soon as they arrived in Cyprus, Vladimir went to the American Embassy and asked for political asylum. The em-

*Iva Najdrovsky, a Czechoslovakian refugee*

bassy was sympathetic, but since Cyprus has an agreement with Czechoslovakia to return defectors, the family was sent to Greece to wait until refugee status in the United States could be arranged. The process took five months. The family managed to survive because Vladimir found a little work as a commercial artist and Iva cooked in a hotel.

Now, in America, the long process of building new lives is just beginning for the Najdrovsky family. The children are in school, doing well, learning English and making friends. Vladimir has not been able to get much work yet as a commercial artist, but he thinks that will change as he learns English and learns more about life in America. Iva is working with a firm of architects.

"It was hard, very hard, to walk away from the friends of a lifetime and from all of the things we owned," she says, "but it had to be done. We always wanted to live in a democracy, and that is why we thought of America. It is good to be here."

# V

---

# IMMIGRATION
# IN THE FUTURE:
# HARD QUESTIONS,
# NO EASY ANSWERS

---

A MERICA is becoming the dumping ground for all the poor people in the world."

"America needs the energy and ideas of new people just as much as it ever did."

"The only way we can keep illegal aliens from crossing the border is with guns, barbed wire, and dogs."

"Illegal aliens are just doing the kinds of work Americans won't do anymore."

"Immigration was great when this country was young. There was lots of land and not enough people then. That's all changed now. There are too many people and not enough jobs."

"America is a humanitarian nation. If we stop taking refugees and immigrants, we will stop being a great nation."

"You can't eat humanitarianism!"

Anyone who listens to a debate on immigration today will hear statements like these and others that are much more emotional. One thing is certain. From coast to coast, Americans are becoming increasingly concerned about immigration. The cover of a recent issue of *U.S. News and World Report* pictures the Statue of Liberty holding a huge stop sign instead of the torch of welcome. The cover story is entitled "Will U.S. Shut the Door on Immigrants?" It reports a widespread belief on the part of American workers that immigrants, particularly refugees and illegal aliens, are hurting the job market because they are willing to work for lower than standard wages. The story quotes a California lawmaker who says that people are angry. "They want us to build a wall around the U.S., pull up the gangplank and say 'no more immigrants.' "

In 1981 the Reagan administration proposed a number of immigration bills that would make it easier for the government to control the flood of undocumented aliens coming into the country. One of these proposals would have given the President the power to declare an "immigration crisis" and seal U.S. points of entry to incoming ships suspected of carrying illegal aliens. Congress did not act on any of those administration proposals, but Senate and House subcommittees have been carefully studying all immigration matters.

While there may be no immigration crisis yet, there are compelling reasons why the United States should be concerned about immigration today and why it should develop an immigration policy that is the right one for the decades ahead. The most immediate reason is that immigration into the United States today is approaching the high levels reported in the early years of the twentieth century.

All indications are that high levels of immigration will continue throughout the decade of the eighties and beyond if U.S. immigration policy remains as it is today. The chief reason why a continued high level of immigration can be expected is population growth in the Asian and Latin-American countries from which most immigrants to the United States come. Projections show that the great majority of these countries will have population increases of from 50 to 100 percent in the next twenty years.

Unemployment, food shortages, and generally poor economic and social conditions brought on at least in part by population pressures almost certainly will cause increasingly large numbers of people to want to immigrate to America and other industrially developed and prosperous countries. Political instability in parts of Asia, Latin America, and Africa can be expected to create serious refugee crises in the future.

Other countries that have been receptive to immigrants in the past—England, West Germany, Sweden, and Australia, for example—are now beginning to tighten their immigration policies. This can be expected to put increased pressure on the United States to take still more immigrants.

The American public's concern about immigration covers a wide range of issues. Job impact is no doubt the most serious concern, particularly in times of high unemployment, but there is little hard evidence to make clear how much immigrants affect the job market. Studies have shown, however, that about 50 percent of all legal immigrants eventually take white-collar jobs. And contrary to popular belief, other studies have shown that many illegal aliens work in jobs that pay more than the minimum wage. Presumably, some of the jobs would be attractive to American citizens.

Other concerns have to do with providing social services such as education, health care, and welfare. In cities where there are large concentrations of immigrants, particularly illegal aliens, there can be serious problems of finding enough money to pay for these services. This is especially true in the field of education, where special school instruction must sometimes be given in Spanish or other languages besides English. The Supreme Court has ruled that the children of illegal aliens are entitled to enroll in school, just as any other children are. The humanitarian reason for this decision is clear, but it does put a special financial burden on schools in some cities.

Beyond all of these concerns, there are other more complex and long-range questions about immigration. They involve questions about the eventual size of the U.S. population and about the racial and other ethnic proportions of our society. Dr. Leon F. Bouvier, Director of Demographic Research and Policy Analysis at the Population Reference Bureau in Washington, D.C., is a specialist on U.S. immigration. In a recent interview he talked about how immigration might affect the number and kind of people who will make up the United States. Here is what he had to say.

*Question:* Dr. Bouvier, just what is the relationship between immigration and the size of a country's population?

*Answer:* Well, there is nothing mysterious about that. The population of a country grows in just two ways. One way is through what we call natural increase. Natural increase is the number of babies born minus the number of people who die. If the number of babies born outnumber people who die year after year, the country's population is obviously going to get bigger.

The other way a country's population grows is through immigration, the number of people coming into a country to live, minus emigration, the number of people leaving a country with no intention of returning to live. If more people come in than leave, you have *net* immigration.

Those are the only two ways a country's population grows—natural increase and net immigration. There's no other.

*Q:* What about the relationship between natural increase, immigration, and the U.S. population?

*A:* Historically, both have been very important. From 1800 to 1900 about 42 percent of the country's population growth came from immigration, 58 percent from natural increase. For most of the twentieth century natural increase has been considerably more important than immigration in population growth, but now that is changing.

*Q:* Can you explain?

*A:* You know that immigration into the United States today is near the high levels of the early twentieth century, if we take both legal and illegal entrants. At the same time U.S. fertility—the number of babies being born—has declined in recent years. In fact, fertility is now below replacement level. Replacement level is the level necessary to keep the population from eventually declining—if there is no immigration.

*Q:* But there is immigration, lots of it, you said.

*A:* Exactly. And today immigration accounts for close to half of all U.S. population growth. If fertility stays as low as it is now, sometime in the next century *all* population growth will come from immigration.

*Q:* What is the significance of these changes?

*A:* They could dramatically change what we "look like" as a nation. What I mean is that if all or even most U.S. population growth comes from immigration in the future the racial and ethnic proportions of the country's population will be very greatly changed.

*Q:* Changed in what way?

*A:* If current demographic behavior continues—I mean if

fertility and immigration stay the way they are now—in less than a hundred years 40 percent of the U.S. population will be post-1980 immigrants or their descendants. Perhaps 80 percent of these will be Hispanic or Asian in origin. Since relatively few immigrants come from Europe and even fewer from Africa, the proportion of Hispanics and Asians to "Anglos" and blacks would increase greatly.

*Q:* Is that necessarily bad?

*A:* I didn't say it was bad. Maybe it will be very good. I don't know. I'm a demographer, not a social or political philosopher. But if it keeps on the way it is going now, there will be change, big change. That's the point I'm trying to make.

*Q:* Can you be more specific?

*A:* Well, I've already been pretty specific, but let's look at two possibilities. We'll call one of them the Status Quo or Let's Keep Things the Way They Are Society. The other we'll call the Multicultural Society.

The Status Quo Society would keep the present racial and ethnic composition of the country very much as it is now. The dominance of the Anglo culture would be maintained, but it would accept influences from other racial and ethnic cultures, just as it has always done. English would continue to be the dominant language, and the laws of the land would remain those that have developed out of our English heritage. At the present fertility level, immigration would have to be reduced *very sharply* to maintain the Status Quo Society.

The Multicultural Society would be one in which racial and ethnic groups will maintain their own cultures and languages much more forcefully than they do now. In some parts of the United States, Spanish, Chinese, and some Indo-Chinese languages might replace English as the number one language. The dominance of the Anglo culture will gradually disappear. I'm not talking about some strange new kind of country. This functioning together of different but more or less equal racial, ethnic, religious, and social groups under one government is called "pluralism" and it has been happening in other parts of the world for a long time. And it will happen here if U.S. fertility stays as low as it is now and immigration stays at anywhere near its present level.

*Q:* What do you think is really going to happen, Dr. Bouvier? Is the United States going to have a Status Quo Society or a Multicultural Society?

*A:* If fertility levels stay the same as they are now, the United States will have to reduce immigration to 250,000 or less per year to have a Status Quo Society. That is about 80 percent less immigration than we have now. That would be very hard to do. There are so many pressures on Congress to keep high immigration levels that they are almost impossible to resist.

No, the chances are that we are moving toward a Multicultural Society. If we continue the present pattern of low fertility and high immigration, we will have a Multicultural Society before we know it.

*Q:* One last question, Dr. Bouvier. You keep saying *if fertility stays low.* What if it doesn't stay low? What if fertility rises? Wouldn't that change everything?

*A:* Of course, it would. If Americans had more babies, immigration would be less important in the racial and ethnic makeup of the country. Some economists think fertility levels may start back up again before too long. I have doubts about that. But remember, whether people decide to have babies or not have babies are very personal decisions. These decisions are made on the basis of how much money the husband makes, whether the wife decides to work, whether they think they can afford a house with two, three, or four bedrooms, whether they think they can save money for a college education for one or two children. Things like that, real personal things. People do not decide to have babies because they want to see a Status Quo Society preserved.

But you are quite right. If fertility rose to just above the replacement level, even fairly high immigration would not make much difference in the racial-ethnic proportions of the country. *However,* such a fertility rise coupled with high immigration would mean that the population of the United States would almost double within a century and that it would keep on growing for long after that. Then the country would have an entirely different set of demographic problems. Would you like to discuss those?

*Interviewer:* Not today, Dr. Bouvier. But thank you very much.


THE PRESSURES for high immigration that Dr. Bouvier referred to are very real. The strongest pressure perhaps is the desire of millions of immigrants already in the country to have their close relatives here with them. The pressure of poor Mexican job seekers on a long, easy-to-cross border is constant. Some U.S. businesses want the inexpensive labor that immigrants, legal and illegal, provide. The desire of refugees for a safe haven makes the United States especially attractive. Hopeful immigrants everywhere still see the United States as the most desirable place to live and raise their children.

But as we have seen, these pressures for high immigration are now coming into conflict with nationwide concern about the levels of both legal and illegal immigration. National public opinion polls show that a majority of Americans all over the country are in favor of reducing all kinds of immigration, legal, illegal, and refugees.

Of 4.5 million permanent resident aliens—legal immigrants all—who reported their addresses to the INS in 1980, over 70 percent lived in just six states: California, New York, Texas, Florida, Illinois, and New Jersey. These states also have high concentrations of illegal aliens. Some of these states have expressed special concern about the large numbers of immigrants living within their borders.

In May, 1982, the Senate Judiciary Committee overwhelmingly approved a bill that would make some important changes in U.S. immigration laws. The bill is being sponsored in the Senate by Republican Senator Alan K. Simpson of Wyoming and in the House by Democratic Representative Romano L. Mazzoli of Kentucky. Here are some of the main features of the bill:

—Employers who hire workers they know are illegal aliens will be fined up to $2,000 for every illegal alien hired. If there is a continuing practice of hiring illegals, the employer can be put in jail for up to six months. People applying for jobs will be required to show proof that they are citizens or legal immigrants.

—Illegal aliens who arrived in the United States before January 1, 1978, can apply for legal permanent immigrant status. Illegal aliens who arrived in 1978 and 1979 can apply for temporary legal status, which might in some cases become permanent. Anyone who arrived illegally after 1979 will be deported.

—Legal immigrants will be limited to 425,000 per year, including immediate family members. Since immediate family members have not been included in past ceiling limits, this action will reduce the number of legal immigrants by about 100,000 per year.

—Immigrants from any one country will be limited to 20,000 per year, just as in the past. The only exceptions are Canada and Mexico. In those two cases the limit will be 40,000 each and if either country does not use its full quota, the other can.

—The limit on refugees will be decided by the President in consultation with Congress.

Clearly, the main feature of the Simpson-Mazzoli bill is to stop or greatly reduce illegal immigration. Persons who have studied the problem are agreed that about the only feasible way to stop illegal aliens from coming into the country is to make it impossible for them to get jobs. The belief is that if employers know they will be fined or even jailed for hiring illegals, they will not do so.

Great opposition to this plan has already developed in the American business world. Many business leaders argue that employers should not have to be policemen. They say that it is the government's job to stop illegal immigration, not the job of American business. Hispanic groups oppose the plan because they fear that it will be used as an excuse by employers not to hire Latin Americans. The idea of a person having to present legal identification documents when applying for a job is strongly objected to by some people. The issue is a very emotional one.

In August, 1982, the Simpson-Mazzoli bill was passed by the Senate by a strong 80–19 vote. The bill has made much slower progress in the House of Representatives, however, and by the end of 1982 had not been put to a vote. The bill's eventual passage by the House and its being signed into law by the President seem likely but by no means certain.

MOST AMERICANS know about the importance of immigration in their nation's history. Most personally know immigrants who have arrived in recent years, like those described in this book. They know that for the most part these new Americans are making or in time can make a useful contribution to the country. But as America moves toward the year 2000, it is clear that future immigration is one of the most pressing and important issues that its citizens must deal with.

The task will be to develop immigration policies and laws that are as humane as possible but that hold the flow of new arrivals to levels that Americans feel are in the best interests of their country. Compassion and control. Those are the goals. They will not be easy to achieve.

# Index

## THE AUTHOR

Brent Ashabranner has written several books on subjects of social importance to the United States, including *Morning Star, Black Sun: The Northern Cheyenne Indians and America's Energy Crisis,* as well as five books for young readers based on his experiences in Africa and Asia. His interest in immigration stems from several years he spent as a Ford Foundation population program officer, during which time he was concerned in part with migration studies. He is presently on the board of trustees of The Population Reference Bureau, one of America's foremost private demographic organizations.

Mr. Ashabranner now lives in Virginia, where he continues to write and consult on overseas development projects.


## THE PHOTOGRAPHER

Paul Conklin is the author and photographer of *Choctaw Boy* and *Cimarron Kid* and has provided photographs for other juvenile books, including *Child of the Navajos.*

Mr. Conklin holds a degree in journalism from Wayne State University and a master's degree in history from Columbia University. He lives in Washington, D.C., and has traveled throughout the world on photographic assignments.

Most recently, Paul Conklin collaborated with Brent Ashabranner on the highly acclaimed *Morning Star, Black Sun.*